ASSIGNMENT: SPORTS

For Syd—
With all the best,
in admiration,
Bob

REVISED AND EXPANDED

ASSIGNMENT: SPORTS

by Robert Lipsyte

A Harper Trophy Book

HARPER & ROW, PUBLISHERS

Several of these articles were originally published in *The New York Times* in different form. © 1963, 1964, 1965, 1966, 1967, 1968 by The New York Times Company. Reprinted by permission.

"Season's End" was originally published in *The New York Times.* © 1971 by The New York Times Company. Reprinted by permission.

Library of Congress Cataloging in Publication Data
Lipsyte, Robert.
    Assignment: sports.

    Summary: A sportswriter discusses some of the various sports events he has covered and includes interviews with several athletes that attempt to reveal the private person behind the public image.
    1. Sports—Addresses, essays, lectures—Juvenile literature. [1. Sports. 2. Sports journalism] I. Title.
GV707.L55 1984   796   83-48436
ISBN 0-06-023908-5 (lib. bdg.)
ISBN 0-06-440138-3 (pbk.)
First Harper Trophy edition, 1984.

Designed by Barbara Fitzsimmons
10 9 8 7 6 5 4 3 2 1
Revised Edition

To the memory of James J. Kernan, teacher—
the man who said Go

Contents

CONTENTS

Introduction
to the Second Edition

The purpose of this second edition is to bring *Assignment: Sports* up to date without losing its historical value. The stories for the first edition were assembled in 1969, while I was a sportswriter for *The New York Times.* Fourteen years later, when I revised and expanded this book, I was reporting on sports personalities for the CBS television network.

Of all the changes in sports between 1969 and 1983, none was so significant as the emergence of the woman athlete, coach and sportswriter, thanks to the women's movement and Title IX legislation.

This change is reflected dramatically in *Assignment: Sports.* There were few women athletes in the first edition. In those days, most women were in cheerleading or "helper" roles, like the wife of the young hammer thrower who was thrilled with his victory over Harold Connolly.

In the second edition, we meet Harold's former wife, Olga Connolly, also an Olympic gold medal winner, and their daughter, Merja, who may someday win a medal of her own. We also meet Tracee Talavera, the gymnast; Bobbi Gibb, the marathon runner, and Nancy Lieberman, the basketball player who benefited by having Billie Jean King as a role model. I've never written a story about Billie Jean that I thought was worth putting in a book. Too bad. She's one of the most important athletes of all time.

As you read these stories, I hope you'll be filtering them through your own knowledge and attitudes. When you read about Muhammad Ali, for example, think about what has happened to him in recent years. Are all great sports celebrities doomed to decline and fall? Do you think it should change the way we think about his early accomplishments?

When you read about the 1968 Olympics, the so-called "problem Games," consider the lessons they offered—then and now—and all the problems that are still with us. Black American athletes are still exploited—although a few of them are making millions. South Africa is still governed by the vicious laws of Apartheid. Rereading the section about the Vietnamese team in 1968, I wondered how many Central American countries now at war would be sending teams to the Olympics just to prove they were still on the map.

Among my favorite people from the first edition are the wheelchair sprinters. They raised my consciousness. There are organized groups fighting for the rights of the disabled now. Those athletes in Bulova Park were brave pioneers.

In 1969, people who ran or worked out regularly were called "health nuts." These days, the roads are jittery with joggers watching out for bikers, and the tennis and racquet ball courts, the softball fields, the swimming lanes are more crowded than ever before. Men and women and children know that sports can make them healthier and happier.

I didn't make too many changes in the first edition. I

dropped a couple of stories that seemed stale, and I pruned a few others. I lengthened the sections on Ali and Dick Tiger. I added a column that I wrote after the first edition of *Assignment: Sports* was published. It's called "Season's End," and it's special to me, one of the last columns I wrote for *The Times* before I left in 1971.

I checked on some of the people who appeared in the first edition. Casey Stengel and Joe Medwick and Rogers Hornsby are dead. Joe Namath, like many former athletes, is trying to make it as an actor, and Ron Swoboda, like many former athletes, is making it as a TV sportscaster. Harry Edwards is still fighting the good fight; in fact, we get to meet him again in the second edition.

I never found out what happened to John Pappas. Did he go back to school, get a new job; is he happy, does he remember his Mets tryout with joy or sadness? If you're reading this, John, drop me a line—maybe there will be a third edition.

Robert Lipsyte
Closter, New Jersey
September, 1983

ASSIGNMENT: SPORTS

SPRING

For the sportswriter, the cycle of the seasons begins in late February in California or Arizona or Florida when the baseball teams open their spring training camps. Technically, it is still winter. But everyone's dream is fresh, all hopes are possibilities, and the year is suddenly new and green.

The New York Mets' first spring training, in 1962, was my first major assignment as a sports reporter for The New York Times. I had been on The Times for nearly five years, restless for a big story. After graduation from Columbia College in June, 1957, I answered an advertisement for a copyboy in The Times' sports department. In September, 1959, I was promoted to reporter; but I spent almost all of my time in the office, at night, rewriting press releases and taking other reporters' stories over the telephone. I rarely got more than a mile from the office on assignment, and then only in an emergency.

One day, the sports editor, James Roach, asked me if I would like to go to Florida and cover this brand-new baseball team, the Mets.

Would I?

I

John Pappas
Tries Out for the Mets

John Pappas appeared on the second day of spring training. He was thin and pale, and he looked about seventeen years old. He said he was twenty-one and that he had come to St. Petersburg, Florida, to be a pitcher for the New York Mets. Nobody knew what to do with him.

In any other major league clubhouse that spring, the equipment manager or the assistant trainer or maybe even the bat boy would have heaved John Pappas out the door. But this was the second day of the Mets' very first spring, and no one was sure enough of his own job to make a decision about someone else. So Pappas just stood quietly in the hushed, green-carpeted clubhouse, his sneakers under one arm, his glove under the other.

Out on the field, a collection of strangers with hopes was trying to sort itself into a team. Rabbit-quick rookies made impossible leaping catches—always when the coaches weren't looking—and the older players, some of whom had once been stars with other teams, tried to sweat themselves down into shape for the long season ahead. The borderline players worked hardest of all, running extra laps around the outfield, taking long turns in the batting cage, and chattering "Attaboy, baby, show him the hummer, good hands, chuck it in there," because Casey Stengel, manager of the Mets, had a reputation for favoring players with spirit and hustle. The borderline players knew if they didn't make it with this brand-new team they would probably slide right on out of the major leagues.

Pappas stood for a long time in the clubhouse, politely but firmly telling anyone who asked that he had no intention of budging until someone from the Mets gave him a tryout. Finally, a tall sad-faced man came out of a side office and looked into Pappas' steady brown eyes. He introduced himself as John Murphy, an official of the new club.

"Where are you from?" asked Murphy.

"New York City," said Pappas.

"When was the last time you threw a ball?"

"Last Sunday, in New York," said Pappas.

Murphy's eyes narrowed, and he smiled, a triumphant little smile. "It snowed in New York last Sunday."

Pappas nodded. "Yes, sir. But not underneath the Triborough Bridge."

Murphy's eyes widened. He motioned Pappas to a wooden bench in front of the lockers and sat down beside him. The young man said he had bought four regulation National League baseballs and pitched them at a painted square on a concrete wall under the bridge. After he was satisfied, he ran for several miles in a nearby park. Then he packed for spring training.

He had arrived in St. Petersburg at three o'clock that morning, he said, after his first airplane trip. It was also the first time he had ever been more than a hundred miles from his parents' home in Astoria, Queens.

Murphy listened and nodded and pulled at his long, sad face. Then he stood up. "We're not holding tryouts here, John." He pointed through the open clubhouse door to the practice ball fields. "There would be a million guys out there if we were."

"I don't see a million guys out there," said Pappas seriously and softly. When Murphy shot him a hard glance to see if he was being smart, Pappas looked down at his black pointy shoes.

Murphy sighed. "You play high-school ball?"

"My high school didn't have a team, Mr. Murphy, but I played Police Athletic League ball. I don't remember which precinct."

"Did anyone ever say you were professional material?"

"No, sir."

"Do your parents know you came down here for a try-out?"

"No one knows, Mr. Murphy."

Murphy sat down again, and his voice became gentle. "Do you go to school?"

"I was going to City College at night, but I stopped going to classes. And I quit my job. I was working in a furniture store. I told my mother I was coming down for a week's vacation and then I'd look for another job."

Almost wearily, Murphy said, "This is not a tryout camp."

7

Pappas took a deep breath. "Mr. Murphy, I don't have much experience, and I'm willing to spend a few years in the minors. But I think I can pitch, and I want to find out now. I want to succeed in the world, and I can do it if I set my mind to it."

"Of course you can," said Murphy, "but there are many ways to succeed in the world besides major league baseball."

"I'm going to stay here until someone looks at me pitch," said Pappas, running a bony hand through his black pompadour. "If they tell me I'm no good, I'll just finish my vacation and go home and set my mind to something else."

Murphy stared at Pappas for a long time. "Okay, John," he said. "You get yourself a catcher and a place to throw and call me up and I'll come over and look at you."

They shook hands, and Pappas, smiling now, bounded out of the clubhouse. "Thanks, thanks a lot," he called back over his shoulder. "I'll see you soon."

Murphy watched him go, then shook his head at us and walked back into his office. Another newspaperman turned to me and said, "That's a flaky kid for you. I don't know why Murphy wastes his time."

"What do you mean flaky?" I said. "He might really have it, he might be a star. And who says Murphy could tell from one tryout?"

"Johnny Murphy was once a great relief pitcher for the Yankees," said the other newspaperman, "and I think you're a flaky kid, too."

The weather was erratic in St. Petersburg that week, some-

8

times cool, almost always windy. John Pappas ran in the mornings near his motel and found youngsters to catch his pitching. Three days after he first showed up, a local newspaper arranged for Pappas to use a nearby high-school ball field, and Murphy promised to drive out to watch him pitch. Murphy said he would even bring a professional catcher.

At 3:38 P.M. on February 23, 1962, John Pappas had his chance. While a dozen newspapermen and photographers watched, he strode onto a scruffy pitching mound and put everything in his slight body behind the baseballs he threw at a young catcher from the Mets' camp. Pappas threw for eighteen minutes in silence. He was wild, and he wasn't very fast.

At precisely 3:56 P.M., Murphy walked out to the mound and put his arm around Pappas' thin shoulders. "All you have is guts, son," he said.

They shook hands. Murphy thanked Pappas for giving the Mets a chance to look him over. Very kindly, he told Pappas to forget about professional baseball. Maybe if he were only fifteen years old it might make sense to keep at it, but at twenty-one he had too far to go and too much to learn.

Pappas thanked Murphy for giving him a tryout. He said he was satisfied and now he was going back to New York.

"I always would have wondered," said Pappas, "but now I know. I just wasn't good enough. Now I'll look for something else, some other way of being somebody."

The ball field slowly emptied, and soon there was just Pappas, and two or three of the younger newspapermen who had secretly hoped that this thin, sallow, round-shouldered young clerk would turn out to have an arm like a bullwhip, a live fastball that hummed, and a curve that danced in the sun. I think we were more disappointed than he was, and we were talking mostly for ourselves on the ride back to town, telling Pappas that there were other ways to succeed in the world besides major league baseball and that he was way ahead of the game; after all, how many men actually get a chance to try out, to find out once and for all? Pappas nodded and agreed and smiled and thanked us for our encouragement.

It was dusk when we reached his motel. The last time I saw John Pappas he was framed in the car window, and he said: "You know, I'm sorry they didn't give me a chance to hit. I'm not a bad hitter. And I play the outfield too."

II

Lobby-Sitting
with a Tough Old Pro

One night in St. Petersburg during the Mets' first spring training season, Rogers Hornsby leaned toward me, his thin lips a scar across his square face, his eyes a hostile ice-chip blue. "You planning on writing an article about me?"

I said that I was.

"You better quote me right," he said. "I'll read it, and if I don't like it, I'll be on your back so fast you won't know what happened."

Satisfied that he had intimidated me, Rogers Hornsby relaxed in an overstuffed lobby chair. It was a normal weekday evening during spring training, and Hornsby was holding court in his normal weekday-evening hang-out—a hotel lobby. He was sixty-six years old then—tall, straight, husky, and vigorous—and his hobby, as listed in the Baseball Register, had remained the same for forty-five years—lobby-sitting.

"I'm easy to get along with if you're on the up-and-up," said Hornsby in his flat, cold voice, "but I'm not a good mixer. I get bored at parties, and I bore other people. I don't like to get dressed up and go out. I enjoy the right kind of people, my kind of people, but I don't like to do the sociable things. I think it's undignified, a man of my age going around

11

in short pants, for example, and I don't think I'm old enough to play golf. I'm used to other people chasing balls I've hit. Damned if I'm going to run after a little ball myself."

Sitting in the lobby, hard and cold, Rogers Hornsby still looked the man who hit baseballs other people chased. Once he had been the most feared batsman in baseball, and many of his records still stand—official records for batting championships in the National League and the top single-season average of .424, and unofficial records for tactlessness, arrogance, and discourtesy.

One night, for example, when he was a player with the Giants, he was having dinner with a teammate, Ed Farrell. Someone stopped at the table and asked Hornsby if the Giants had a chance to win the pennant that year.

"Not with Farrell playing shortstop," snapped Hornsby.

Hornsby was soon sold to the Boston Braves as a player-manager. Early in the season he was asked if the Braves had a chance to win the pennant that year. Hornsby gestured contemptuously at his players.

"These humpty-dumpties?"

So on he went, from team to team to team. In 1952 he lasted exactly half a season with the St. Louis Browns. When the owner, Bill Veeck, fired Hornsby, the players chipped in and bought a silver trophy for Veeck. On it was inscribed:

TO BILL VEECK FOR THE GREATEST PLAY SINCE
THE EMANCIPATION PROCLAMATION, JUNE 10, 1952,
FROM THE PLAYERS OF THE ST. LOUIS BROWNS

But Hornsby got in the last word. Of Veeck, he said: "When you work for a screwball, you got to expect screwball tactics."

Rogers Hornsby returned to the big leagues in 1962 as batting coach for the New York Mets in their first season. His reputation had preceded him, and some of the players were a little worried. Was he still the arrogant old Hornsby, impatient with any man whose talent was less than his had been, or had he mellowed with time?

On the first day of batting drills, an outfielder named Joe Christopher ran up excitedly and blurted: "It's a great pleasure to meet you, Mr. Hornsby. For years I've been carrying around a magazine article with your batting tips."

The players around the batting cage edged forward to eavesdrop. They tensed when Hornsby snapped, "Did the tips help you any?"

Christopher said, "I didn't have anyone to work out with before."

Hornsby allowed himself a faint smile. "You'll get all the help you want now. Just holler."

The players relaxed. Hornsby had mellowed.

"How come," I asked him in the lobby that night, "you seem to have so many enemies in baseball?"

"Wouldn't want them phonies for friends anyway."

"But so many people call you narrow, bigoted, suspicious, and old-fashioned."

"Maybe because I'm not two-faced," said Hornsby. "I'm

sure no diplomat. I say what I mean. Always did. From the start."

He had started in another era, born in a cattle town, Hornsby's Bend, Texas, where his grandfather had battled Indians and rustlers. He was raised in North Fort Worth after his father died. Baseball was a way out of the small town, and young Rogers followed his brother Everett, a spitball pitcher, into the Texas League. Everett never went much further, but in 1915 the St. Louis Cardinals barnstormed through Texas and were impressed with Rogers, a thin nineteen-year-old second baseman. They bought him for five hundred dollars, and they called him up to the big leagues that September.

"Hornsby," said the Cardinals' manager, "you're too skinny. I'm gonna have to farm you out on account of your size."

In baseball language, "farmed out" means sent to the minor leagues for further experience, but young Rogers thought it meant he would have to go to a farm. So he spent that winter on his uncle's farm in Lockhart, Texas, sleeping twelve hours a day and consuming great portions of ice cream, steak, milk, cheese, and potatoes. When he reported back to the Cardinals in the spring of 1916, he weighed one hundred and sixty-five pounds, thirty-five more than the previous season. He hit .313 that year—the first step toward the Hall of Fame.

Rogers Hornsby never smoked, because "cigarettes cut down your wind." He never drank, because "highballs are bad enough, but beer goes right to the legs and slows you up." He never went to movies, because "it might affect my batting eye." And he never stayed out late with girls.

"I gotta get my sleep," he would explain. "The people pay money to see me at my best, not tired and hung over. I go out with girls—I'm human—but I figure if I don't get the pitch I want between 7 P.M. and midnight, forget it. I'll always get another chance to go to bat."

He never smoked or drank or stayed out late, but he had three wives, he was named in another man's divorce action, he punched a few men in the mouth, and he spent a great deal of money betting on the horses. Rogers Hornsby was no saint. But there was no doubt that he was devoted to baseball.

"Baseball is my life, the only thing I know and can talk about, my only interest," he said that night in spring training, his ice-blue eyes flicking around the hotel lobby. "People ask me what I do in the winter when there's no baseball. I'll tell you what I do. I sit and stare out the window and wait for spring."

Rogers Hornsby died a few years later, and when I heard of his death, I remembered him in his lobby chair, as tough as the oak and leather, no free smiles or diplomacy. And I remembered him standing stiff and solid by the batting cage, cold eyes shaded by yellow-tinted sunglasses, watching ball-players who would never be half the batter he was but would make their way through life with greater ease. I remember one of those young players, in a friendly mood, pleasantly

15

saying to the old coach, "What would you do, Mr. Hornsby, if you got in a batting slump?"

Hornsby snapped, "When you have a lifetime average of .358 you don't have any slumps."

III

A Columbia Rower
Pulls His Weight

When the ice breaks on the rivers of the north, rangy college men go down to the sea in fragile wooden peapods, determined to pull their weight. The sport, of course, is rowing, and the eight oarsmen and one coxswain in each racing shell are called the crew. Probably no other team sport in the world demands as much blind dedication, physical energy, and animal courage—and offers as little material reward and public recognition.

Richard Arthur Hansen was twenty-one years old in the spring of 1962. He had been rowing for Columbia for four years. His devotion had cost him most of the accepted by-products of college life: the dormitory bull sessions, the midnight parties, the casual flirtations over coffee. He could not care less.

"Years from now when I look back at college," he told me one afternoon on campus, "I will remember most the crew —the guys that I rowed with—and the days on the water. And that's what I'll miss most too."

Dick Hansen was born in suburban New Jersey. He played no sports at Hasbrouck Heights High School, spending his spare time clerking in a grocery store. He won an academic scholarship to Columbia College, and when he arrived he

17

was 6 feet 1 inch tall, and 200 pounds fat.

During Freshman Orientation Week that fall of 1958, an assistant crew coach buttonholed him as he wandered, bewildered, around the campus. "How would you like to come out for crew?" asked the coach, impressed with Hansen's height.

Hansen barely knew what the man was talking about, but he said, "Yeah, sure. Why not?"

He had time to regret his words. A week later he was sitting in a sixteen-man barge, pulling a 12-foot oar through the garbage-littered Harlem River. He was drenched in the wake of passing sight-seeing boats, peppered from shore with rocks thrown by small boys, and harassed by coaches who yelled "Pull harder" just about the time he was telling himself "Dick, you're crazy. You hurt all over. You don't have to put up with this."

But he did. In late fall, the crew moved indoors. Three times a week, Dick ran three miles and went through an hour of muscle-wrenching calisthenics and then two or three ten-minute sessions in a simulated shell in the underground tank, trying to remember how his sliding seat worked, how to bring the blade of the oar back parallel to the water, and trying to forget the torn skin on his palms.

In late February, when the ice broke on the Harlem, the Columbia crew went outdoors again for spring practice. There were only twenty-seven heavyweight freshman left of the forty-five who had started. Now it was six days a week on the water, two hours a day of looking at the sweating back in front of him and wondering if he could keep rowing when his hands turned blue.

In the late spring, Dick made the Number Two position in the first freshman boat. He held it for three weeks before the stroke from the second boat beat him out for the slot. Dick was standing on the shore, a substitute, when his teammates competed in the big International Rowing Association regatta that June.

Dick lost more than thirty pounds his freshman year, barely got to meet any Barnard College girls, gave up all between-meal snacks, and always got to sleep by midnight on Saturday night. For what?

"It was wonderful then, and it still is," he said, his deep-set blue eyes faraway. "When eight guys are pulling together in unison and you see the puddles go by and you can tell that everybody is giving everything he has and the shell just seems to lift out of the water . . . well, you know everything is right with the world."

Between his freshman and sophomore years, Dick spent the summer clerking at the grocery store and exercising. In his second year at Columbia, he made the varsity.

"I'm part of a bunch of guys who've found out they can drive themselves long after they're exhausted, guys who've stuck it out. I've learned about everybody pulling out all the way, because the guys get ticked off if you don't pull your weight. It just means somebody else has to pull a little harder."

Crew members are clannish. They meet in the evenings for

19

tea and a verbal re-row of races and practice. They have their private jokes; their own greetings. Together they ignore the boys who quit the crew, and they tolerate the rest of the world.

After his graduation, Dick Hansen and the other seniors on the varsity would probably never row again. But he will probably tell his children someday of the tradition and mystiques of the crew. He may tell them about the mythical oarsman who slumped over his sweep near the end of the race and gasped, "I can't row another stroke." The rower behind tossed him overboard.

His children will laugh at the tale—but for the wrong reasons. Hansen and all those who have rowed know the story is absurd: No oarsman would ever quit unless he were dead.

IV

Short Takes
with the Champ

MIAMI BEACH, February 18, 1964—He was stretched out on a rubbing table, his chin propped on his fists, smiling at himself in a locker-room mirror. "You are beautiful," he said.

The steam from open shower stalls fogged the mirror and curled the pages of our notebooks.

"But what if you lose, Cassius; what happens then?" asked a columnist from Los Angeles.

"So beautiful," he said as his image faded in the steam. "Your publicity has overshadowed your talent. You are the double-greatest."

"Let's be serious for a minute," insisted a sportswriter from Boston. "What if the champ beats you?"

Cassius laughed into his fists. "I won't feel bad. I'll have tricked all the people into coming to the fight, to paying two hundred and fifty dollars for a ticket when they wouldn't have paid one hundred dollars without my talk."

"So this whole act," said the Boston man, "is just a con job, eh?"

"People ain't gonna give you nothing no way; you gotta go get it." He pushed up on the table, and his eyes sparkled. "I'm making all this money, the popcorn man making

21

money, and the beer man, and you got something to write about; your papers let you come down to Miami Beach where it's warm."

The Boston man seemed a little angry at that. "Exactly what are you going to do when Sonny Liston beats you after all your big talk?"

"If Liston beats me, the next day I'll be on the sidewalk hollering 'No man ever beat me twice.' I'll be screaming for a rematch." The big brown body relaxed and seemed to melt into the rubbing table. The voice dropped to a whisper. "Or maybe I'll quit the ring for good. I'm twenty-two years old now." He closed his eyes. "I think I'm getting tired of fighting."

* * * *

MIAMI BEACH, February 25, 1964—All evening, rumors swept the city that Cassius was not going to show up, that he had taken the step from hysteria to madness, that even now he was at the airport, waiting for a flight to Mexico City. Actually, while the rumors were at their height he was standing quietly in a far corner of Convention Hall, waiting for his brother, Rudy, to make his professional boxing debut.

Few people noticed him. He was wearing a tight-fitting black tropical suit, a black bow tie on his ruffled white dress shirt. He was surrounded by his trainers and aides and friends. Only once, in the second round when his brother knocked Chip Johnson down, did Cassius open his mouth. "That's it!" he yelled.

At the end of the fourth round, when it was announced that Rudy had won his first professional fight, Cassius turned abruptly and followed a squad of Miami policemen with pearl-handled guns to his dressing room.

I went to my seat at ringside, where another reporter told me he did not believe Clay was en route to Mexico after all, he was still in his hotel room hiding under the bed.

* * * *

NEW YORK, June 26, 1964—The long, black air-conditioned Cadillac limousine moved through Harlem, its dual speakers pounding out Marvin Gaye's version of "What's the Matter with You, Baby?" All the way down Lenox Avenue we stamped our feet and clapped our hands—the new champ, now known as Muhammad Ali; his brother, Rudy, now known as Rahman Ali; and their old friend from Louisville, Ronnie King, whose Muslim name was Omer Bey.

"Who is the champ?" sang out Muhammad.

"You is the champ," Rahman sang back.

"Who is that?"

"Muhammad Ali."

"Who's gonna be champ when Muhammad Ali retires?" sang out Muhammad Ali.

"I'm gonna be champ," Rahman sang back.

23

"But you ain't gonna fight Muhammad."

"No, sir!"

"You say he's too fast," sang out Muhammad.

"Too fast," Rahman sang back.

"You say he's the greatest."

"The greatest."

"You say you can't handle him."

"No, I can't handle him."

The limousine stopped at a red light, and Muhammad asked the chauffeur to play the Marvin Gaye record again. We rolled down all the windows, and when three pretty girls walked by, we started stamping our feet and clapping our hands again and singing along, "What's the matter with you, baby?"

* * * *

STOCKHOLM, August 6, 1965—"Man, you just can't go strong all the time," he mumbled into his pillow, "can't be such a controversial figure, dodging all these traps . . ."

The hotel room was in Sweden, but it could have been anywhere: his clothes and boxing equipment strewn around the room, the portable stereo record player and a stack of 45's on the bureau. He had just fought an exhibition match at an amusement park in the city, and now, at midnight, he was tired from the boxing, the traveling, from the mounting pressures of his life.

24

"Just be myself." He was mumbling into the pillow, barely audible above the music of the record player. "Go out among the little people, the children and the folks sitting in garbage alleys, and they say 'That really you, Champ? You know you couldn't pay Chubby Checker and Joe Louis to come here and talk to us like you do.'

"That's what makes you powerful, the little people."

He kicked off his shoes and dug his toes into the mattress. "I live right and catch all this hell, don't drink or smoke or chase bad women. I treat everybody nice. You know, nobody ever came to me and said 'I'm going to become a Muslim because you are.' You have to live it and practice it and sacrifice and study. You don't love the cereal because Willie Mays eats it, but you might try it because of the man. But then you got to do the thing . . ." His voice began to trail off. "Life is a dream, boo-boo, boodey-boo . . ." and he was asleep.

* * * *

LAS VEGAS, November 23, 1965—In the days leading up to the fight, Floyd Patterson had proclaimed himself an instant knight, a crusader fighting beneath the banners of Integration, Christianity, Goodness, and America who would wrest the heavyweight championship from the Black Muslim Ali. It was hard to feel sorry for Patterson when Ali, who had been careful not to reply in kind, took it out on the crusader's hide.

It was the cruelest fight I ever saw. For twelve rounds, until the referee stopped it, Ali mocked and humiliated and punished Patterson like a little boy pulling the wings off a butterfly, piecemeal. Throughout the fight Ali screamed "No contest, get me a contender" and "Boop, boop, boop" as his lightning jabs flicked out a little pain at a time. Whenever Patterson seemed about to collapse, Ali would let up the attack, giving the man time to recover enough to suffer some more.

The morning after the fight the two men sat side by side at a press conference, and Ali said to Patterson: "You should get honors and medals, the spot you was on, a good clean American boy fighting for America. All those movie stars behind you, they should make sure you never have to work another day in your life. It would be a disgrace on the government if you had to end up scuffling somewhere."

* * * *

MIAMI, February 17, 1966—In the late afternoon when the air was sluggish and sweet, Muhammad Ali sat beneath a palm tree in front of his rented home and called to the passing children. He had finished working out for the day, and now, as the children came, the tension drained from his round face.

"Hey, little girl in the high-school sweater, you not gonna pass me by today."

"Hi, Cassius, how you been?"

"Fine. Whatcha learn in school today?"

The telephone rang inside the house. One of the three Muslim sisters who cooked for the champion and his entourage answered it. She called Ali to the phone. He went reluctantly.

When he returned, I saw that his face was twisted with rage.

"How can they do this to me?"

"What's that?"

"How can they reclassify me 1-A without another test to see if I'm wiser or worser than last time? Why are they so anxious? Why are they gunning for me?"

The sweetness drained out of the afternoon as red trucks from the television networks pulled up in front of the house, as the telephone rang continually, as reporters and photographers piled out of cars.

He jumped out of the lawn chair. "I've got a question," he said. "For two years the government caused me international embarrassment, letting people think I was a nut. Sure it bothered me, and my mother and father suffered, and now they jump up and make me 1-A without even a test. Why did they let me be considered a nut, an illiterate, for two years?"

No one had the answer for him. A television newscaster asked him what he thought about the war in Vietnam. Ali shrugged.

27

"Do you know where Vietnam is?"

"Sure," said Ali.

"Where?"

He shrugged.

"What do you think about the Vietcong?"

Ali shrugged again. "I got no quarrel with them Vietcong."

* * * *

LONDON, May 18, 1966—We were drinking tea in the Picadilly Hotel when three young black men with precise British diction, who said they were medical students, stopped by our table. They asked Ali to take his time beating up Henry Cooper in the championship match three days later. They asked Ali to please inflict suffering before knocking the white man out.

"And you're doctors?" asked Ali, setting down his teacup.

"We hope to be."

"Where you from?"

"He and I," said the spokesman, an intense chunky young man, "are from British Guiana. That one is from Ceylon."

"That right," said Ali, leaning back in his leather-covered chair. "Now, why you want me to hurt Cooper?"

"All this talk about Cooper's left hook and how he is going to knock you out," said the chunky youth, shaking with anger.

"Oh, that," said Ali, grinning. "That's good."

"Good?" sputtered the medical students, so loudly that all the polite tea-drinkers looked up.

"Look here," said Ali. "You got to talk up a fight, say how vicious and dangerous this Cooper's left hook is, how the champion is scared—"

"But, Mr. Ali," said the young man from Ceylon, "he did knock you down last time."

"I was talking to the fans, not paying Cooper no attention," said Ali, brushing it aside. " 'The champion is scared,' the sportswriters write—they got to write something— 'about this vicious left hook.' Now you got it?"

"You mean," asked the chunky student, "that Cooper does not possess a superior left hook?"

"It's all right," said Ali, shrugging. "The fans read what the sportswriters write about Cooper's vicious and dangerous left hook, and they start saying 'Man, we got to see this fight; this cat is going to knock the great Ali out.' They go and buy tickets, which cost money which go in my pocket. Now you got it?"

"In other words, Mr. Ali," said the Ceylonese carefully, "you approve of all this talk."

"You got it."

"Thank you, Mr. Ali," said the three students, moving away. They looked completely confused.

* * * *

HOUSTON, February 5, 1967—The karate-trained Fruit of Islam carefully searched everyone entering the Muslim mosque, especially the half-dozen white reporters and photographers. Our ball-point pens were taken apart; nail files were confiscated. This is necessary, the Muslims teach, because the truths of Elijah Muhammad are so strong they can drive men crazy.

Raymond X, minister of the mosque, introduced the main speaker as "another of Elijah's ministers and the heavyweight champion of the world in that world." He gestured toward "that world," a drab Black neighborhood beyond the auditorium window.

"Al-salàm, Alaykum!" said Muhammad Ali.

He told an audience of several hundred—most of whom were non-Muslim Blacks curious to meet him—that the teachings of Elijah had made him champion. Heredity and talent had made him a good fighter, but the Muslim teachings had kept him living clean and free from temptation. He turned to the blackboard and conducted a lesson on the evils of eating pork.

"The swine is the nastiest animal in the world," he said, "a mouthful of maggots and pus. They bred the cat and the rat and the dog and came up with the hog."

He then drew a sketch of a pig and imitated its snuffling noises. He also told the audience that "dumb Negroes come out dumber Negroes" after worshiping in Christian churches. He said that Jesus Christ was dead, but the Muslim God, Allah, was a living man.

30

"Other churches preach pie in the sky when you die," he said. "We want something sound while we're around on the ground.

"I enjoy lecturing to you about the Honorable Elijah today more than I will whipping Ernie Terrell tomorrow."

After he had been speaking about fifteen minutes, the white newsmen were asked to leave.

* * * *

NEW YORK, March 22, 1967—"Are you tense before a bout?" asked a man with a microphone a few minutes after the noon weigh-in for the fight with Zora Folley that night.

"Always tense, sometimes scared," snapped Ali, stomping off in his slush-stained work boots.

The broadcaster hurried after him. "Are you scared now?"

"Yup, scared," said Ali. "Anything can happen in a fight. Might trip going into the ring and break my arm."

* * * *

CHICAGO, April 26, 1967—A spring storm lashed the city, and sheets of rain poured out of a bleak gray sky and roiled the waters of Lake Michigan. Through the plate-glass window of a motel coffee shop, Muhammad Ali watched the storm and moodily picked at three poached eggs on his plate.

"You think they'll give me poached eggs in jail?"

"I don't think so."

In two days he was scheduled to report to the Houston, Texas, draft-induction center. He would go, but he would refuse to take the one step forward that would turn him into Private Cassius Marcellus Clay, Jr. We wondered what would happen then. Would he be arrested on the spot and dragged off to jail, or would that just be the opening scene of months, maybe years, of legal maneuvers? And what would happen to his heavyweight title?

He had been up early that stormy April morning, arranging to store his gray Cadillac in a local garage and close out the motel room he kept as his Chicago home.

"I don't want to go to jail," he said, still staring out the rain-streaked window, "but I've got to live the life my conscience and my God tell me to. What does it profit me to be the wellest-liked man in America who sold out everybody?"

"Why don't you skip the country?"

"You serious? How long you been around me? I got to stay here and lead my people to the right man, Elijah Muhammad."

His tone was so absolute I felt slightly embarrassed. "Well, you've talked about someone so poisoned with hate he'd kill you and think he was doing the country a favor. It wouldn't serve any point, your getting killed."

Ali shook his head. "Every day they die in Vietnam for nothing. I might as well die right here for something."

Someone else at our table asked, "What about just playing

32

the game like other big-time athletes? You wouldn't be sent to the front lines. You could give exhibitions and teach physical fitness."

Ali leaned across the table, his eyes suddenly bright, and he spoke very firmly. "What can you give me, America, for turning down my religion? You want me to do what the white man says and go fight a war against some people I don't know nothing about, get some freedom for some other people when my own can't get theirs here?"

Breakfast stretched into lunch as people came to our table, some to sit and talk, others merely to shake Ali's hand and wish him luck. Most were white men. Toward noon Ali's mood brightened, as the storm outside passed over the lake. The champion's eyes softened, and his voice deepened and dropped. He was going to play back a vision.

"Ah-lee will return," he intoned. "My ghost will haunt all arenas. The people will watch the fights, and they will whisper: *Hey, Ali could whip that guy . . . You think so? . . . Sure . . . No, he couldn't . . . Wish he'd come out of retirement.*"

His voice sharpened. "Twenty-five years old now. Make my comeback at twenty-eight. That's not old. Whip 'em all —if I get good food in jail. Don't you think?"

A newcomer to the table said it was all so very sad that such a handsome and gifted young man should have to contemplate death and imprisonment. Ali straightened, his eyes bright again, eyes of a martyr, reflecting the licking flames.

"Allah," he said, "okays the Adversary to try us. That's how he sees if you're a true believer."

He smiled. "All a man has to show for his time here on earth is what kind of name he had. Jesus. Columbus. Daniel Boone. Now, Wyatt Earp . . . who would have told him when he was fighting crooks and standing up for his principles that there'd be a television show about him? That the kids on the street would say 'I'm Wyatt Earp. *Reach.* ' "

He half closed his eyes. His head lolled back. "Two thousand years from now," he whispered. And then he softly began to sing:

> *Muhammad Ali, Muhammad Ali,*
> *He roamed the Western Hemisphere,*
> *He was courageous and strong,*
> *He called the round when the clown hit the ground.*
> *Tell little children whatever they believe,*
> *Stand up like Muhammad Ali.*

* * * *

SAN FRANCISCO, April 27, 1968—The sweet stench of marijuana floated out of the crowd in Civic Center Plaza and through the open windows of a blue Oldsmobile 98. The man behind the wheel, Jerry X, turned to the men in the back seat and said, "You could get stoned just breathing the air around this place."

Ali rolled his head, pretending to be stoned, and giggled in a strained falsetto. "Ladies, and, uh, gentlemen . . . we got a race problem in . . . uh, you got to excuse me, I'm as high as a kite."

Captain Jerry laughed and snapped another picture of Ali. Minister Majied smiled indulgently, but C. B. Atkins, a New York booking agent, stared out at the peace rally in the plaza, now swelling to about twelve thousand young people, and said, "I'll get you on right away so you don't have to wait."

"No," said Ali, "I'll wait for my time."

Captain Jerry laughed sharply. "Muhammad Ali, you'll wait for your time? The man is going to see you get time— time in jail."

A rock band finished its set on the wooden platform, and a man began shouting about peace in Vietnam. Ali shook his head. "I'm out on government bond; you not going to catch me talking about no war or draft-card burning or stuff like that. No, sir, I'm—Hey, look at those cats out there. There's one looks like he wants to raise some—Hey, there's one with plaits in his hair. My, oh, my. And look, I think I see one of the Smith Brothers."

"Smith Brothers?"

"Yeah, off the cough drops," said Ali, slapping his thigh. "No, I must be wrong; he got too much hair."

A bearded youth on a bicycle spotted Ali and rushed over, thrusting his hand through the open window. "Let me shake the hand of the only true heavyweight champion of the world."

"They made me bigger by taking my title," said Ali. "Be-

35

fore, the little man on the street couldn't identify with me. He'd say 'You not with me; you up on the hill with Whitey.' "

"Mr. Ali," said a Black man, leaning into the car, "let me thank you for sticking up for Black America."

"There are only two kinds of men," said Ali, "those who compromise and those who take a stand."

"You are beautiful," said someone out of the crowd engulfing the car. "You ever going to fight again?"

"Yeah, I'll be doin' the Ali Shuffle again someday. Excuse me now. I need some quiet to study my speech."

He chuckled softly as Captain Jerry expertly eased the big car through the crowd, out of the Plaza, and onto a sidestreet. "I don't say we shall overcome," said Ali, "because I done overcame."

He pulled a heavy black briefcase initialed *M. A.* onto his lap. "This is my boxing gloves now," he said, opening it and riffling through books and tape spools until he found a thick sheaf of oversized white index cards on which Ali and his young Muslim bride had lettered his speech. In blue ink, written across the top card, were his opening words: "We have a serious race problem here in America."

The speech lasted twenty-five minutes. The crowd, basking in the golden sunshine, was friendly but not particularly moved. Ali's delivery, high-pitched and severe, contrasted with his firm and glowing good health. It was hard for the crowd to take him seriously when he said that he had come as a representative of Elijah Muhammad, the man who could save the country with his program for orderly racial separation.

There were very few light moments in the speech. The crowd laughed only once, when Ali said, "Now, you sport fans, when I told you a man would go in five, you put your money on it. You know I never been wrong. I missed my prediction on Sonny Liston by one round, but he was no fool, he stayed on his stool."

The crowd applauded when Ali said, "Black is beautiful," but he lost them when he said, "Now I'm gonna drop the bomb. I don't mean to offend you integrated couples, but we believe that mixed marriages should be prohibited."

The crowd lost its good nature then, and hooted and booed, and began to drift away from the platform in the echoing plaza.

Back in the car, C. B. Atkins, the agent, said, "You'll have to modify the speech for such a radical audience."

"I was too strong for them; they couldn't take it," said Ali.

"You see that naked man out there?" asked Captain Jerry.

"Where?"

"While you was speaking he was just walking around, buck-naked."

"I don't believe that," said Ali, looking at Minister Majied, who just smiled and nodded.

"Buck-naked. I got a picture," said Captain Jerry. "Man, this is California. They got love-ins out here."

"I don't know nothing about that; don't want to hear about that," said Ali, thumbing through his speech cards.

37

"But I saw them walk away. I had too much strength for them. People just can't stand the truth. They want to hear about violence or integration, but they can't stand the truth that can save them."

* * * *

NEW YORK, August 7, 1969—At lunch, Ali said, "Look around. You see people eating good, dressing good, probably living better than me. You don't have to be a boxing champ to have a good life. That's something I just learned the last few years. I have a pretty young wife now, and a thirteen-month-old daughter and another baby five months on the way. Hope it's a boy. Doctor says my wife can have ten. Like to have three before I go to prison. Not afraid of going to prison. Read somewhere they have ninety percent Black men in prison right now. Nothing's going to happen to me in prison. But there might be riots in the country when they put me away."

He seemed relaxed and in good trim for a twenty-seven-year-old out of training and caught up in the busy pace of campus speeches, conventions, and television shows. We took our time walking over to the television studio. He enjoyed the people who stopped him on the street to shake his hand.

The show was "What's My Line?" and he was the mystery guest. *Sign in, please.* He had been on the show five years before, and the panel had guessed his identity immediately. He had just beaten Sonny Liston for the first time then. This time he said he was going to trick the panel. While a makeup man applied powder, Ali made faces at himself in the mirror and practiced his mystery-guest voice, a high piping "Yiss" and a squeaky "Neeoo."

"Hey, champ, you know what you sound like?"

Ali simpered, "I'm not a girl, I'm champ of the worl'."

But when he went out on stage, he used a gruff deep voice, saying "Nope" and "Yup."

The panel did not guess his identity. It did not even come close.

We took our time strolling back to his hotel, the Hilton. The sun was warm, and people smiled at him. He said he felt good these days. He said he could handle anything that came up. His appeals of a conviction for draft evasion were not going well, he said, and he thought he would be jailed; but his case would stand as an example to the world that there were forces in America determined to keep him from spreading the truth. He said that many Americans, particularly Black athletes, were saying "If they can get Ali, they sure can get me too."

We went up to his room. His key did not fit the door's lock. The hotel had locked him out of his room. He did not seem perturbed, and after a few telephone calls we went down to the hotel's credit department.

Matter-of-factly, a man behind the credit desk asked for the $53.09 in charges billed to Ali's room, and told him that in the future he would have to pay room service in cash. The assistant manager told me that Ali's credit was poor in New York hotels. Apparently, hangers-on had run up bills in his name that had never been paid.

Ali peeled off a fifty-dollar bill and a five-dollar bill. The security detective who took us back upstairs and opened the door with a special key asked for Ali's autograph.

I said, "For a lousy fifty bucks they locked you out of your room."

"This don't bother me none," he said, starting to pack for the flight home to Chicago. "Word probably got around, he's not the champ no more, he's busted, you better get your money up front. That's the way it is. When you the champ you can sign and sign and sign and sign."

* * * *

NEW YORK, March 9, 1971—He was as cool in his first professional defeat as he had ever been in victory. The morning after he lost to Joe Frazier he sat in his hotel room and said: "News don't last too long. Plane crash, 90 people die, it's not news no more a day after. My losing not so important as 90 people dying. Presidents get assassinated, civil rights leaders assassinated, you don't hear so much about that no more. World go on, you got children to feed and bills to pay, got other things to worry about. You all be writing about something else soon. I had my day. You lose, you lose. You won't shoot yourself."

40

I reminded him that the first time we ever met, seven years ago in Miami Beach, he told me that if Sonny Liston beat him he would demand a rematch, he would be on the sidewalk hollering, "No man ever beat me twice."

He grinned and winked, then closed his eyes and began to chant: "Fight him again . . . I'll get by Joe this time . . . I'll straighten this out . . . I'm ready this time . . . You hear me, Joe? . . . YOU HEAR ME? . . . Joe, if you beat me this time you'll really be the greatest."

V

Before the Derby:
Forward Pass Is Restin' Easy

Two stout women from St. Louis, their white hair damp and limp from the heat of the noon, peered into the darkened stall. One of them said, "Hi, boy, how are you feeling today?"

When the horse didn't answer, the other woman turned to the groom, Dan Barnette, and asked, "What do you call him?"

"Forward Pass," said Barnette.

"Do you call him Forward or Pass?" asked the first woman.

"I just put 'em together. I call him Forward Pass."

"Oh, thank you," said the women, disappointed. They waved good-bye to the horse and trudged heavily back to their car.

"Sometimes," whispered Barnette, winking and spitting simultaneously, "I call him you-big-son-of-a-bitch, but I say it sweet, and he just yawns; that's his good-humor sign."

The big horse lay down in his stall, legs gathered beneath his glossy body, his head cocked as if in rumination.

"See him in there, restin' easy; he don't give a damn how many people bettin' on him, how much money, or nuthin'," said Barnette. "Tonight when we draw the hay and give him only grain, he'll know he'll be racin' tomorrow, but he won't

42

know if it's an overnight or the Kentucky Derby."

Barnette, a small, wizened, bandy-legged man with light bright-blue eyes, began working as a groom for Calumet Farms in 1939. In 1941, he groomed his first Kentucky Derby winner, Whirlaway.

"Whirlie, I called him. I could go in his stall and lay down right with him. He'd walk two or three times around me, then lay down too. I could put my hand in his mouth, he wouldn't bite me. Naw, I don't think about him much no more. Like you lose your dog, you don't keep thinking about him."

Another Calumet Farm horse, Pensive, won the Derby in 1944, but Barnette was in the army in Europe. After the war, Barnette came back and groomed the great Citation, whom he called Cy.

A skinny, nervous young man, perhaps eighteen, walked into the barn and joined us. We sat and talked about the army, and the boy said he had been in Vietnam only twenty-nine days when a mortar blew him up. He had just been released after nine months in the hospital.

"I got wounded in France," said Barnette, dropping into a cloth chair.

"Shrapnel or mortar?" asked the boy.

"Pistol. Thirty-eight caliber."

"Wow," said the boy, "that musta really tore you up. Close combat, huh?"

"Naw," said the old man, spitting. "Accident. 'Twas one of ours."

Barnette got up and started picking around Forward Pass' stall. "After a while, horse gets confidence in you. Gets to be a real easy job. After you get a horse under control, he won't bite you, wheel on you, savage you. Always did like the studs. Used to say 'Don't give me no more of them sourpuss fillies.'

"Yep, easy life. No, never been married, though I've acted like I was on occasions. Younger grooms comin' in now are a different breed, just want to do their work and get on out; they don't care about horses no more."

He scratched the white stubble on his shapeless jaw. "Well, hell, whole world like that. You looka those gippies, what you call them, yeah, hippies, smokin' on weeds while they're deliverin' the U. S. mail."

Barnette peered in at Forward Pass. He seemed satisfied. "He don't know what's goin' on. Whole world goin' crazy, he don't give a damn."

VI

The Pear Says:
"I Am Swoboda"

This friend, an architect, went to Shea Stadium one night and
sat through some of a twilight-night double-header between
the New York Mets and the Houston Astros. His wife and
two small children had left for a vacation in the country, he
said, and he felt at loose ends this Tuesday evening. And so,
without dawdling unnecessarily at the office, he arrived during the early innings of the first game, long before the lights
went on and while the jets trailed black streaks across a
bright powder-blue sky.

He did not notice the jets. He was busy watching Nolan
Ryan's fastball begin to lose speed, and he hunched into a
sitting crouch when Ron Swoboda came to bat in the bottom
of the ninth inning. The Mets were trailing 3–2. There were
two out. The count ran to three balls, two strikes; and the
architect, as he later admitted, began knocking nonexistent
dirt from spikes he wasn't wearing. It was a live and unre-
hearsed drama; Swoboda struck out and ended the game.

"You know," said the architect much later, over a beer,
"I think this is why baseball is still the national pastime. I
am Swoboda. I've tried very hard to be Fran Tarkenton or
even Joe Willie Namath, but I don't even know how far back
they draw their arms to pass. Some friends of mine skated

45

in a private school in Massachusetts, and they can be Bobby Orr, but not me. And as for soccer, I don't even know what the ball feels like. But I am Swoboda."

The architect rubbed his finger in the wet rings his beer glass had left on the wooden table. "Let me tell you about my greatest day in sports. I was thirteen years old and very fat. The kids in school called me The Pear. I guess they thought I was shaped like a pear.

"Well, one day about this time of year, late spring, our class was scheduled to play for the school championship, and the captain got appendicitis, and the second baseman's father pulled him out of school to take a trip, and the left fielder threw a book at the teacher. He lost his eligibility.

"I was in a small class, and there were only three substitutes on the team. I was the third. The assistant captain requested permission to field an eight-man team, and when the teacher said No, the assistant captain requested permission to play a girl. The teacher said No. So The Pear opened in right field.

"The first time I came to bat, the assistant captain, whom I did not like by this time, told me just to get a piece of the ball. I swung very hard, three times. The third time I swung, the ball was already in the catcher's mitt, the assistant captain told me.

"Things went better in the field. Only two balls were hit to right field, and the center fielder ran over and caught them both. The second time I got up, the assistant captain told me to wait the pitcher out and get a walk. I struck out, looking.

46

"We played seven-inning games, and the third time I got to bat was the bottom of the seventh. Two out and the bases empty. The score was 1–0, theirs. The assistant captain asked special permission to skip me in the batting order or have a girl pinch-hit. The principal was there, and he said No. The assistant captain threw his glove over the fence and cried.

"Well, the first pitch was a called strike, and the second was a ball. I could tell since it bounced before it reached the plate. I closed my eyes on the third pitch and swung from the heels and showed them where I lived. The assistant captain was screaming for me to hold up at first, but I went into second standing up. I would have been out, but the second baseman got rattled and dropped the ball.

"The leadoff batter came up, and he grounded to shortstop, an easy out; but I was running now, really steaming along, and when the first baseman saw me run, he started laughing and dropped the ball. I turned third and kept on going home.

"The assistant captain was screaming for me to go back to third, and so were both teachers and the principal and all the girls, but I just kept going. I remember very vividly seeing the catcher take the throw from the first baseman and crouch in front of the plate and grin at me and the last thing I thought was, Make way for The Pear. I think you would have had to be very fat once to understand how much I enjoyed running that catcher down.

"He wasn't able to hold on to the ball after I hit him, of course, and I scored, and the leadoff got to third. He came

47

home on a single, and we won the game, and everyone shook my hand or kissed me. Even the assistant captain made a little speech."

The television set over the bar was dark by now; the Mets had long since lost the second game of the doubleheader 6–5. The architect, very satisfied and slightly high, got to his feet. "This sport," he said a trifle pompously, "is dull and contrived and made complicated by algebra whizzes who never measured up to their early promise. But it lives because I am Swoboda."

SUMMER

I like my job best when I'm traveling somewhere new to talk with people I've never met before. I've gotten to most states and major American cities. In 1965 I spent the summer reporting on sports in Europe, and in 1967 I went to the Soviet Union.

Sportswriters travel as much or more than any other newspaper specialists, but rarely spend much time in one place. The baseball writer is in a city for three or four days at a time, for example, and spends a great many hours getting to and from the airport, the hotel, the stadium, and the only restaurant in town that serves dinner at 1 A.M. after a night game.

The two foreign assignments offered me the added luxury of being able to spend weeks in a single city. I was also able to meet foreign sportswriters, who sounded amazingly like American sportswriters. We talked—sometimes through interpreters—about all those days and nights we spent on the road, chasing stories from town to town and hoping our luggage and stomachs would catch up.

I

A Norwegian
Fishing Guide and His River

The Laerdal River is fifty miles long, boiling out of the mountains of southwestern Norway and down into the great Sognefjord, where it meets the salmon and the sea trout fighting their way upriver to spawn. The final fourteen-mile stretch of the Laerdal is considered some of the best sport fishing in Europe, and it is said to have swallowed the lures of more dukes and princes than any other river in the world.

For most of his life Olaf Olsen has guided the rich of the pools where the trout skulk, to the swift currents that carry the salmon. He has tied dry flies for Prince Harald of Norway, just as his father did for Prince Axel of Denmark, as his grandfather did for the English lords who once controlled the river.

"I love this river, it is my life," said Olsen one summer afternoon. "I have fished all of it. The river holds no secrets from me."

He stood, small and brown and gray-haired, on the rocks along the Hunderi Pool, his favorite sea-trout beat. We watched one of his clients, a lanky Norwegian businessman, cast clumsily into the gin-clear water. The businessman had booked Olsen's services more than a year ahead of time. Like

51

most sport fishermen, he looked both uncomfortable and blissfully happy.

It was still early in the afternoon. A warm sun hung over the river, filling some of the shadows in the valley between sheer, purple-gray mountains. Twice, Olsen's client snagged his line on some bushes behind him, and each time the little guide freed it. "Ah," breathed Olsen as a brown shape moved in the water and "ah" again as the client cast out at it. The brown shape moved on, and the client grinned sheepishly.

"You must strike it exactly, precisely, hard and quick," said Olsen, "not a long pull, but sharply, just as you see him begin to disappear. It is not easy."

"Not for me, it's not easy," said the client.

"Once," said Olsen, "a great salmon came into this pool, a salmon at least seven inches longer than the largest I ever caught, which was fifty-four pounds. This salmon arrived on the seventeenth of July and stayed until the fifth of September, the day the season ended.

"He always lay in the middle of the pool. There was no difficulty reaching him. Every day I fished for him, with every kind of tackle I knew. And he just lay there and made fun of me."

"Of you?" said the client.

"Yes," said Olsen, "and he was only a salmon, who is not nearly as intelligent as a sea trout."

Smiling, the client went back on the rocks and began to cast again.

"Olsen," bellowed the client, suddenly struggling with his rod.

The guide moved quickly onto the rocks, taking the rod from his client. His stubby brown fingers danced over the rig, ripping off the fly, replacing it, untangling the reel. Then he straightened up and began to move his arm, slowly at first, and life seemed to flow from his shoulder and through his wrist and into the 8½-foot fishing rod, moving it like a whip, the green line snaking out into the water, hitting, moving, then coming back as the rod and the arm became one.

Olsen began to smile, and the client shook his head with wonder. Then Olsen stopped, as if suddenly remembering that he wasn't there to fish. He returned the rod to the client and walked back to where we had been standing, away from the rocks so our shadows would not frighten the fish.

"I am fifty-three years old," said Olsen, "and only once have I left Norway. Last year I went to Scotland to fish with a group that comes here every year. We caught fifteen salmon. I caught thirteen myself."

He lit his pipe. "But this is my river, my life. Once a Canadian came, a very rich man with a bad heart, and he lost two salmon in a row. We rested, then tried again. The salmon struck, and just as it leaped out of the water my client fell over. With one arm I caught him, with the other I fastened the rod to a fence. Then I ran for the doctor, and we took the Canadian to the hospital. He was dead.

"Two hours later I came back, and the salmon was still on the line. I played him slowly and brought him in. Often I have wondered how I thought to fasten the rod at such a time."

Such thoughts Olsen usually reserves for the long winter,

53

most of which he spends in the basement of his neat, cozy house in the town of Laerdal. There, with his seventy-six-year-old father, his twenty-five-year-old son, and two other Laerdal *ghillies,* or guides, Olsen ties the dry flies which are sold under his name throughout Europe. From October until May it is sunless and cold in the valley of the Laerdal, and Olsen aches for the season.

"I have cold thoughts in the winter," said Olsen. It was nearly evening now, and the client had gone back to his hotel. Olsen and I were sitting in overstuffed chairs in his living room. "There are four hundred nets on the Sogne Fjord, put out by commercial fishermen. The nets trap ninety percent of the fish before they get to the Laerdal. In the winter I worry about that.

"I worry about the hydroelectric station they will build in the mountains someday. I am afraid it will slow the water and change the river. What will happen to the fish?"

He sighed and tamped fresh tobacco into his pipe. "Well, the Swedish poachers came. I chased them away. The Germans occupied our valley in the war, and I was able to convince them not to fish. Farmers put nets on the Laerdal; we got new laws to stop them. All the young men leave the town to work at an aluminum factory, but my son stays with me on the river."

The guide smiled. "But those are winter thoughts. This is the season now, the best time for me. Even with such a poor fisherman for a client, it is the best time. I can stand in the sunshine and watch the fish and look at my river."

54

II

Down Among
the Hammer Throwers

They were waiting for Harold Connolly at the awards stand, glancing at their watches, digging their shoe tips into the stubbly grass of Randall's Island, squinting through the bright June sunlight at cars moving along the Triborough Bridge overhead.

"Maybe Connolly just went home," one of them said. "You know, this is everything to Harold."

"It's a matter of sportsmanship," said Ed Burke, the winner. "You can be an animal in the ring, that's all right, but afterwards . . ."

The third-place finisher, Tom Gage, couldn't stop smiling. A recent Cornell graduate, he had just thrown the hammer 215 feet 2 inches, the best throw of his life, good enough to put him right behind the great Harold Connolly at this championship track meet in New York City. Connolly, the veteran Olympic star, had won this event nine times in the past eleven years. But this day's throw, 218 feet 12 inches, was only good enough for second place.

"Harold will show up," someone said. "Maybe he just went to take a quick shower."

"He should be here now," said Ed Burke.

Burke was not smiling. His throw, 220 feet, was not the

best of his career, but it had been good enough to beat the great Harold Connolly. Now some of the pleasure of his victory began to drain away as he stood in the hot afternoon sun with nothing to do but wait for Harold.

It was a big day for him, Burke told those of us who asked, but he kept glancing over our shoulders for the burly figure of Connolly. Burke was twenty-six years old, a history instructor at a California junior college who had begun throwing the hammer as a student at San Jose State. He had been a discus thrower then, and the coach thought that Burke's arms were a little too short for the platter-shaped discus but just right for the hammer, a 16-pound steel ball at the end of a long wire.

Burke, a powerfully built six-footer with sun-bleached hair, switched to the hammer. The hammer was going to take him to the 1964 Olympics in Tokyo, he told a pretty blond classmate named Shirley, who used to watch him practice the vicious twisting windups of the hammer throw and try to tell him what he was doing wrong.

They got married in Ed's junior year, and they worked on the hammer together. Sometimes Shirley would cut her own classes to attend Ed's and take notes for him so he could go to a track meet and photograph the great Harold Connolly with an 8-millimeter camera. At night they would study the films. After graduation, Shirley worked as a secretary while Ed earned a master's degree in international relations.

Ed also asked Connolly if he might practice with him. Connolly said Yes. The story gets a little fuzzy here because

Connolly does not discuss it. Burke says that he asked Connolly what he was doing wrong and the older man said, "You're doing fine; everything's just fine."

"When I got to Tokyo," said Burke, his eyes still searching the field, "I realized that I didn't know how to throw the hammer at all. I don't want to say anything more about Connolly."

The field men compete in their own little pocket of the track world. They may hate each other; they may try to psych each other, but they can really depend only on each other for understanding. Through the long lonely hours of practice that began again for Ed Burke after his poor showing in Tokyo, he inspired himself by thinking about Connolly.

Connolly—thick-shouldered, squat, graying—a schoolteacher with a perpetual half-smile, was very gracious to Burke when they met at track meets after Tokyo. But later on, as Burke's throws got closer and closer to Connolly's, the older man grew more reserved. On the day that Burke won, Connolly sat against a wire fence, like a half-smiling Buddha, watching his young rival throw. Connolly rose slowly for his own last throw of the competition, and when it fell short, he lumbered off the field without a backward glance.

And now we were standing in the sun, wondering if the great Harold Connolly would show up for his second-place medal. Tom Gage was thanking Burke for pointing out a little mistake he was making with his foot, and Burke was saying that he wasn't angry at Connolly anymore, that the man he would use to inspire him now was Romuald Klim, the Soviet thrower who had beaten them all in Tokyo.

"I'm going to get Klim," said Burke. "He's a boastful, haughty, belligerent guy. Every time he wins it's a personal triumph for Leninism or something. Well, I'm going to—"

Burke fell silent, and everyone turned to follow his gaze. Moving slowly across the field, half smiling, freshly showered, and wearing a clean white shirt, was the great Harold Connolly.

Connolly reached the group and nodded to Tom Gage. "Nice going," he said.

"Tom's a real comer," said Burke brightly.

Gage, caught between the two men, shifted his feet awkwardly and said, "We'll see what happens."

Burke turned to Connolly. "How many of these have you won, Harold?"

Connolly shrugged.

Burke grinned at him. "You don't mind letting a kid have one once in a while, do you?"

III

The Caddies
Root for Murphy's Kid

"Your typical, average professional caddie is a broken guy," said Bill Manwaring, a typical, average professional caddie. "We don't have roots, don't have steady jobs. Don't even pay income tax, a lot of the guys. If I was going to do this over again, I wouldn't want to do it. It's all right for young kids. Get some money, go to college. That's why we're rooting for Murphy to win, we're rooting for Murphy's kid."

Murphy's kid was Jeff Albanese, a shy, skinny, high-school sophomore with braces on his teeth. In a month he would be fifteen years old. Because of his age and because this tournament—the $250,000 Westchester Classic in Harrison, New York—was his first professional tournament, his name had been dropped into the caddie pool for the lesser golfers. Two days before the start of the tournament, when he reported to the caddie master for his uniform, he was told he would carry the clubs of Robert Murphy, a twenty-five-year-old rookie from Nichols, Florida.

"I never heard of him," said Jeff. "He wasn't supposed to be so good."

But Murphy opened the tournament with an eight-under-par 64, held his lead the second day with a 69, and came into the final round far ahead of the field. He had needed only two hundred and one strokes for fifty-four holes—fifteen strokes under par and three strokes ahead of his nearest rival, the plodding old pro, Julius Boros. And by Murphy's side, handing him clubs, pointing out the placement of the pins, estimating the yardage, was Murphy's kid.

Caddies these days tend to be high-school and college students, particularly at professional tournaments in the summer when country clubs make an effort to enlist youngsters at the expense of the full-time touring caddies. Jeff Albanese, the eldest of nine children of a Port Chester, New York, electrical contractor, was younger than most, but otherwise he was a typical, average semi-professional caddy.

"We figured," said Manwaring, the typical, average pro, "that if Murphy wins fifty thousand dollars for first place, he'll give the kid twenty-five hundred dollars. Now that's a start toward college."

"I'd buy a car," said Jeff, who was lounging in the sun against the white wooden wall of the caddie shack.

"You're too young to drive."

"I'd save it for a couple of years."

"I'm telling you," said Manwaring, "you go to college."

At 2 P.M. Jeff hoisted Murphy's 40-pound bag of clubs onto one thin shoulder and began the four-and-a-half-hour trudge over the hilly course. To accommodate television, Murphy's threesome was the last group out, and sometimes the entire tournament was trailed by two contrasting figures: the bouncy 210-pound Murphy walking empty-handed, and the staggering 120-pound Jeff Albanese bent double under the bag and the broiling sun.

Meanwhile, up ahead, old Julius Boros, fat and crafty and persistent and impassive, shot a 33 for the first nine holes. Murphy needed an extra putt on the ninth hole, and he lost a chance to stay even with Boros. Murphy shot a 37.

"There's that kid," someone whispered as Murphy and Jeff swung into the back nine. "I read about him in the paper this morning. He's a very young kid, and he stands to make a fortune."

But old Boros came on and finished the round with a 68, which brought his total for the tournament to 272, sixteen strokes under par. Murphy came up to the last hole with a chance to beat Boros by gambling on a long shot, but he played it cagey. The crowd fell silent as Murphy prepared to putt. The hole was fifteen yards away.

If he made it, he would be tied with Boros, and they would play off. If Murphy missed the putt, he would drop into a three-way tie for second place, with Jack Nicklaus and Dan Sikes.

Jeff Albanese's thin face suddenly looked strained. The fifteen-yard putt could be worth the difference between $50,000 and $20,000 to Murphy, and between $2,500 and $500 to Murphy's kid.

Murphy missed.

After it was all over, after Boros got his check for $50,000 and Murphy and Sikes and Nicklaus each got one for $20,416.66, I went down to the last hole and found Jeff

Albanese slumped on a wooden chair in the official's tent.

"How do you feel?"

"Not so good," he said. Then he shrugged. "I'm happy. Murphy's a good guy. He shouldn't have played it so safe on that last hole, and he had some trouble with putts, but it's okay. It's only my first pro tournament."

IV

Athletes in Wheelchairs
Compete for the Paralympic Team

Joanne Keyser, the sixty-yard-dash champion, had just won the first heat in a fierce blond blur, and now some of the young women had gathered along a sideline to discuss their chances. Linda Laury, a buxom, twenty-six-year-old redhead who had never competed before, was flip. "I didn't come to set records," she said. "I came to have fun."

Hope Chafee, a young chemist from Chicago, hefted an 8-pound practice shot, as if to assure them all that sixty-yard dashes were only an afterthought with her, that shot-putting was her game.

But Ella Cox, her long blond hair tumbling onto her tanned arms, was clearly nervous. Keyser had broken her sixty-yard-dash record and taken her championship away a year ago, and Ella wanted it back. "What do you expect?" Ella snapped. "Keyser is all arms and young."

The sun boiled out of a pale-blue sky, making their wheelchairs hot to the touch. Volunteer officials, students from Pace College and Queens College, called out names for the next heat.

Ella and Hope checked out Linda's chair. The 8-inch front casters had been tightened so the chair would stay in its lane during the race. Normally the casters are loose enough to allow the chairs to turn. The brake on Linda's chair had been removed completely for the race so she wouldn't accidentally engage it during her follow-through.

"Here goes," said Linda, still acting flip. She left her purse with Ella, shrugged theatrically, and wheeled out among the tape markers that made a wheelchair racecourse from the rutted asphalt parking lot behind the Joseph Bulova School of Watchmaking in Astoria, Queens, New York.

Beyond the parking lot on a large and grassy field, the archery, discus, shot put, and javelin events of the twelfth annual national wheelchair games moved into the middle rounds. There was a sharp edge to the outdoor competition that summer of 1968, as there had been earlier in the indoor events, the swimming, table tennis, weight lifting, and bowling. Among the nearly three hundred male and female competitors from thirty states were some who had supposedly retired and others who had not been seen since the Kingston, Jamaica, Paralympic Games of 1966, or even the Tokyo Paralympic Games of 1964. Everyone who could make it was in Queens that week, competing for a spot on the American Paralympic Team that was to go to Israel in the fall.

The starter's gun snapped, and Linda got a good start. Her hands moved rhythmically on the outer steel rim of the big back wheels, in short choppy strokes that brought the chair to full speed early. The woman in Lane Two, the bad lane, foundered in a rut; two others lost strength; and Linda, pumping steadily with long coasting strokes, took the lead in the stretch and won.

Ella, who had coached her, laughed and clapped as Linda rolled back into the group. Linda was flushed, and her hands shook with excitement. She took her purse and Hope's 8-pound shot from Ella as her friends rolled out for the next heat.

Ella and Hope also qualified for the next round in Class II competition. This class is mainly for polio victims and others whose handicap places them somewhere between the incomplete quadriplegics of Class I-A, who have serious spinal damage and no abdominal support, and the "walkers" of Class III, who are too crippled to compete in normal athletics but do not necessarily need wheelchairs or crutches in normal life. Everyone in paralympic games, however, must compete from a wheelchair.

Ella Cox, the former champion, had been stricken with polio at five; Hope at eight. Both were twenty-three years old in 1968, and both felt they had had an easier time of it than red-haired Linda. Suddenly and mysteriously, one morning when she was thirteen years old, Linda was unable to rise from the breakfast table.

"Small children make adjustments and friends," said Ella, "and adults, if they don't become embittered, work hard to get their independence back. But teenagers are just at that age when everyone is running off for a pizza, and there's a great tendency to withdraw."

"I had depressions," said Linda, "but not so much over my handicap as over where to go to meet other people like me. I had to function the best I could in an AB world."

"AB?" I asked.

"Able-bodied," said Linda.

Hope nodded and wheeled closer. "You never really know what a wheelchair can do until you see other people doing it."

The three met as undergraduates at the University of Illinois, which has one of the country's finest rehabilitation centers. Ella and Linda, who work for the government in social security administration, live together in an apartment, drive cars, and square dance and bowl from wheelchairs.

"If you're a good gimp, you'll do all right," said Linda.

"Gimp?"

"We like to use that word first, before an AB does."

Ella, Linda, Hope, some of the other competitors, and Ben Lipton, the director of the Bulova School and the guiding spirit behind American wheelchair games, all insist that sports for the handicapped are now more social and recreational than medical, although they were originally developed after World War II for therapeutic purposes. Now, the Vietnam War has created a large new wave of young wheelchair athletes.

Hope and Linda wheeled out again for their last heat, and Ella said, "You know, we consider this sport. We come here to win and have fun. But AB's don't really understand this. Even after you give them some big hairy explanation, it comes out sob-sister for most people. Please, one thing, don't go back and write a sob story about us."

I told her I didn't feel sad at all. She smiled, and we turned

66

to watch the race. Hope drew the bad lane and finished fourth, wheeling back to gather her shot and try to make the team in her own event. Linda, the beginner, placed in the semifinals and wheeled back glowing.

Ella finished her racing day with a stirring second-place finish, behind the unbeatable Joanne Keyser, and then they all moved off to group around a husky hundred-yard-dash man who was leaning out of his wheelchair and saying, "Atlantic City is for old people and cripples. Now, I like Ocean City. That's for me, that's where the action is. How about you?"

V

Casey Stengel
Has a Conversation

"Respect your tools," said Joe Medwick, twisting around in the front seat of the limousine. "That's the first thing I teach 'em. You got a good bat, keep it locked up in your locker, or the pitchers'll use it and break it on you."

"The pitchers will break it on you every time," said Casey Stengel from the back seat.

"And shoes," said Medwick, flush and hearty after whiskey and steak, "shoes is very important. Kids these days don't know how to buy shoes. Shoes got to be tight. You buy shoes cheap and after a rain and a few night games, they stretch, and then you see these kids wearing four socks under their shoes. Basketball socks."

"Terrible," said Stengel. "Y'know, one time I lost a twenty-three-inning game for a pair of shoes. Had a fella on third, stole fifty-four bases the year before, and he run home in the last inning, which was the twentieth, and he stumbled two times and was out.

"So they asked him, 'Last year you stole forty-six bases, and now in the nineteenth inning you stumble two times.' And he says, 'Wall, I didn't figure Mr. Stengel was going to put me in, so I didn't wear my good shoes.' It looked like house slippers he had on. I managed four more years there, and let me tell you I never sent a pinch-runner into the game without first looking at his feet."

"And gloves," continued Medwick, pounding the seat. "I tell these kids to put their names on their gloves, and if I see a glove around loose, I take it and hide it in my locker for a few days and really let them sweat."

"You don't say," said Stengel.

"I heard someone stole Carl Erskine's watch at the party," said Edna Stengel.

"Haw!" exploded Medwick, waving the red box with his own gift watch inside. "First thing I ever learned—you never let go of anything that's got your name on it. Especially at a party."

They lapsed into brief silence. It had been a good party at Shea Stadium, a gathering of old-time Dodgers, Yankees, and Cincinnati Reds. Stengel had welcomed them as "fellows I'm glad to see ain't been buried yet," and Medwick, burstingly proud of having just been elected to the Hall of Fame, was the star of the two-inning old-timers' game played before the regular Mets' game.

Later, the old-timers trooped upstairs to drink and eat and tell stories. They laughed again at the old one about the apocryphal old-timer who was asked, "How do you think you would do in modern-day baseball?"

"I think I'd hit about three-twenty."

The interviewer then asked, "Only three-twenty?"

And the old-timer answered, "Hell, I'm seventy-five years old."

The limousine swept soundlessly on toward the city, and Mrs. Stengel pointed toward La Guardia Airport and whispered to me, "Have the planes been taking off on—"

"Quiet," said Stengel, "I'm asking this man a question. I noticed how you took two strikes and hit the ball to right field."

Medwick puffed up and pounded the seat. "I tell these kids, stupid, you can't swing for the fences, you got to learn to hit to the wrong field, these Drysdales and these Gibsons, you can't swing from down there and expect to hit them."

"We'd come to St. Louis," said Stengel, "and there you were, an hour before anybody else, taking batting practice."

"I sure did."

"I looked at a boy on the Coast, luckiest day of his life," said Stengel. "He went four-for-four and I knew we needed catchers bad, and I said, 'Yes, sir,' and they gave him seventy-five thousand. He ain't done nothin' since. I don't think he *can* do anything, and I have given up looking at prospects for one day only."

The limousine swept into Manhattan, and the driver asked, "Which hotel?"

"The Hilton," said Medwick.

Mrs. Stengel said, "And then go to the—"

"Quiet, the man is talking," said Stengel.

"One year," said Medwick, "I led the league in twelve of thirteen hitting departments, and I expected a sizable raise, and Mr. Rickey cut me by five thousand bucks. I said to him, 'How can you do this?' And he said, 'I expected you to hit three-seventy-four again.' "

"It's enough to make you an anarchist," said Stengel.

"The Essex House, please," said Mrs. Stengel.

70

VI

Croquet: Lawn
Enough and Time

In a corner of London where there was lawn enough and time, Dudley J. V. Hamilton-Miller relit his pipe, hefted the mallet he had used for forty years, since 1926, and slowly, coolly, stalked onto the playing field. He ignored the sudden rain; a croquet match is suspended only when the court is under water.

On the veranda of the Roehampton Club, in green wicker chairs, half a dozen other players watched the tall retired headmaster neatly stroke a wooden ball through a narrow iron hoop.

"A tidy shot, Hamilton-Miller," groaned his opponent, Roger Hicks.

"Perhaps," said Captain H. G. Stoker, who had lost to Hamilton-Miller that morning, "but I have seen him play better."

They fell silent as Hamilton-Miller, his large face impassive, moved about the court, measuring the lie of the four balls with quick flicks of his blue eyes, his mind jumping three, four, ten strokes ahead.

"The end game is tensing," said Captain Stoker. "It is sheer guts; you must keep your courage going."

"Ahhh," breathed the little gallery as Hamilton-Miller's

mallet struck, sending one ball across the court, the other right up to the next hoop. "That's croquet."

There are, at most, seven hundred serious croquet players in England. They pronounce it to rhyme with "smoky," and a few of them can remember the good years, like 1902, when King Edward VII sparked a renascence with his enthusiastic, if erratic, play. Many of them remember tournaments on these very same Roehampton greens when World War II antiaircraft fire rumbled in the background and to stop playing seemed something like a partial surrender to the Axis forces.

Although Oxford and Cambridge have organized croquet teams and several British industrial firms have laid out courts for their employees, the sport suffers from its Victorian image—young ladies in wide, white dresses, blithely toeing a ball toward the hoop on the vicarage lawn when no one was looking. Croquet has also suffered from progress and democracy. A match between two people may take three hours on a rectangle of expensively manicured grass measuring 35 yards long and 28 yards wide. On that same amount of ground, without need for a gardener, dozens of people can play many other games. There are few clubs or private individuals in England who want and can afford croquet courts.

"It's really a pity," said Captain Stoker, who after eighty years could look back over distinguished careers in the Royal Navy, and Wimbledon tennis, and on the West End stage. "Croquet is a godsend in old age; it keeps the doctor at bay."

Over lunch at the club that day Hamilton-Miller had tried to explain his philosophy to me. "Games are not a preparation for life. That's nonsense, it's out of date," he had said. "Games are a part of life."

And that afternoon, his pipe failing in the rain, he was hunched over two wooden balls, swinging the mallet easily between his legs. The little gallery tensed with him.

Smack. Too hard. Stoically, Hamilton-Miller walked off the court.

"Bad luck," said Mrs. V. C. Gasson, who took up the sport after a nasty spill from a horse in India.

"Too bad," said Mrs. Gladys Riggall, who plays winters in Capetown.

"Not a wise shot," said Captain Stoker.

"And now," said Roger Hicks, who had been waiting for this moment, "ready for croquet."

"That's right," said Hamilton-Miller softly. He eased into a wicker chair as Roger Hicks struggled into his waterproofs, picked up his mallet, and strode out onto the court.

Hicks returned a moment later, dejected. He had missed his shot. The rain stopped as Hamilton-Miller stepped onto the court again for his eventual triumph. The clouds parted for the sun.

"Ah, yes," said Captain Stoker, half closing his eyes against the drifting smoke of his cigarette. "If one has to die, what better place, here on a beautiful green lawn in the sunshine—wearing clean white flannels?"

VII

A Soviet Weight Lifter
Describes His "White Moments"

A huge man sits quietly in a small room, a sensual smile on his full lips as he remembers the years when every world and Olympic weight-lifting title was his, the years when he was known as the world's strongest man.

"At the peak of tremendous and victorious effort," he says in Russian, slowly and through an interpreter, "while the blood is pounding in your head, all suddenly becomes quiet within you. Everything seems clearer and whiter than ever before, as if great spotlights had been turned on.

"At that moment you have the conviction that you contain all the power in the world, that you are capable of everything, that you have wings. There is no more precious moment in life than this, and you will work very hard for years just to taste it again."

The huge man sighs. His name is Yuri Vlasov, and he is only thirty-two years old, but his best years are clearly behind him. After his great Olympic triumph in Rome in 1960, the white moments became fewer and dimmer. Now, as we talk in this small room off an air force gymnasium in Moscow in the summer of 1967, Vlasov says that winning became too easy for him, that there was not enough real competition to extend him, to prod him to greater effort.

74

In those years, he says, he began to look for something else. Because he had learned and seen much in "sport's speedy school of life," and because he knew he had a capacity for hard work, he decided he could make a valuable contribution through literature. In 1962, he won a short-story contest sponsored by a Soviet sports newspaper, and soon after the 1964 Olympics, in which he finished second to a younger countryman, Leonid Zhabotinsky, he left competition to write.

Trained as an air force engineer, Vlasov remained in sports as a weight-lifting coach at the Central House of the Red Army, the military sports society. But now his friends were no longer athletes, but other writers. And his heroes now were Tolstoy ("of course"), Hemingway ("how difficult it is to be brief"), Jack London ("very romantic—I know *Martin Eden* by heart"), and Guy de Maupassant ("he too wrote short stories").

Within a few years Vlasov published more than fifty stories, almost all about sportsmen. Some of them were collected in *To Surpass Himself,* a book that earned more than nine thousand rubles (ten thousand dollars) in a very short time.

"I found in sports a very rich field for writing," he says, his eyes steady and challenging behind their thick glasses. "There is tragedy, joy, and fulfillment in sports—the realization that man is master of his destiny no matter the obstacles, that faith must be based on reason and self-confidence, not on the ancient dogma of a church.

"And there is intense emotion after labor and sweat, the salty pleasure of the white moment."

But Vlasov's faith in himself as a writer began to falter. He wondered if the popularity of his work was based less on its worth than on the fame of its author. Did people think he was a freak? He pressed harder in his writing, sometimes shut up in a country cottage, away from his wife and daughter. To prove himself as a writer, he decided, he would write a semi-autobiographical novel that would explain, for all time, the essence of sport: the need of an individual to search for and accumulate strength and power. The book would gain critical acceptance, he believed, and restore his self-confidence.

But the writing went poorly. The early pages seemed artificial to him, and his greatest strength as a writer—the simple vividness of his details—was gone. Desperately he tried to re-create the white moments on paper. But he could not.

And so, in 1966, in an attempt to relieve the physical and emotional tensions building within him, he says, he returned to the weights. He thought that heavy training would restore his self-confidence. But it did not. His progress in the gym was slow and unrewarding.

"I even pity myself for coming back," he says, filling the small room with a gentle heave of his great chest. "I cannot tell people this because it would be misunderstood and considered cowardice. And now, having started, I have a moral commitment to my comrades on the team. I have to stay. Perhaps I should have thought of that before."

He clasps and unclasps his great hands, and there is silence in the room. His coach, several other Soviet lifters, my interpreter, and I stare at the bare wooden floor. We know that Vlasov's last remaining world record was broken a few weeks before by Zhabotinsky, the new strongest man in the world. We know that Vlasov has been moody since then, sometimes disappearing for a day or two at a time without even leaving a telephone number, a serious offense for a Russian officer and athlete. And we know he is training hard for the Spartakiad, the Soviet Union's internal Olympic games, scheduled for later in the summer.

The silence is broken. "Maybe I'll quit for good after the Spartakiad," says Vlasov. "I can't keep postponing my novel, my new stories forever. Sports drains my energy and leaves nothing for writing."

The great shoulders square, and the room shrinks even more. "I could beat Zhabotinsky. I could win the 1968 Olympics. But it is not worth the work."

Then the broad forehead wrinkles up to the receding hairline, and the room grows larger as the huge man sinks back in his chair. "I have to make a decision soon. I must get back to my writing. And yet, if I thought those white moments could ever return . . . Ah, but I am afraid that the pleasure is gone forever and only the salt remains."

VIII

Season's End

Last Saturday, a grain of sand inside one swim fin ground out a shallow, dime-sized hole in my big toe. Bandaged now, the raw spot is only a nostalgic sting, and soon that will be gone, too. The season is over, the sun has lost its savage lick, and the night's edge has sharpened.

On a clear, fresh morning in July we met for doubles in the park. The neighbor's twelve-year-old dropped back as I rushed the net, and his father lobbed one over my head that the boy, surprisingly, hit cleanly. For what seemed like a very long time they played alone, father and son, driving deep shots at each other; the son belted the ball as best he could, the father returned it carefully. Finally, the boy faltered and hit the ball a foot beyond the baseline, but the man played it and drove the ball into the net, smiling. Their partners did not dare say a word, it was too private a moment.

The season is over. But on the day I hurt my toe, the air and water both were warm, and the sunshine filtered through to dazzle the tails of silvery fish that streamed past my face mask in silent squadrons. They showed no quick terror at the net, they merely changed direction like gusts of wind. I finally captured two crabs locked together in love or battle, then threw them back.

78

One dense sweet evening in August, on a public dock in the harbor, the four of us sat like crows on a line and fished. We didn't say a word, but if any of our eyes met, we smiled. Fishing boats churned back from the open water with long, gray shapes dangling from their gin poles. Private cruisers slid past, and reddened, bareheaded men raised cocktail glasses at the sight of us. We fished until it was no longer possible to distinguish the masts thrusting into the dark sky, and the running lights of faraway boats mingled with the stars.

Very early one morning, running along the curve of the water mark, I heard heavy splashing behind me and turned to see a white horse plunging through the shallow water. The horse and rider, a girl in a bathing suit, were silhouetted in the rising sun and I could clearly see only her hair, blond, flowing behind her, dazzling in the new light. They passed and she never turned her head toward me, and then they disappeared behind a dune. I did not see them again that morning, or ever again, and no one on the beach last summer could think of where she might have come from.

One day I played baseball, actually softball, and stood in the outfield high on the smell of freshly cut green grass. I had forgotten how the sharp, clean smell rises in waves, alerting you to the angling line drives that might slice past for a home run. But no one hit a ball to left field all day, and the sun cooked out the fresh clean smell and pinched the hot hairs on the back of my neck, and I remembered, too, the sweet, mindless boredom of long hot days in the outfield.

On the last weekend of summer, the man up the beach finally offered a ride on his Sunfish. A half-mile out the bay turned dark and rough. Waves began to crash over the prow and rake my back with icy tines. An off-shore breeze stiffened, and the man said he was not sure he had the tacking technique to get us back without capsizing. I liked him for that and told him not to worry, we were both strong swimmers, and he held the rope in his teeth as he turned the sail, and the Sunfish leaned over and bucked through the chop while we laughed and hollered all the way home.

But the season is over now. The nets sag on the tennis courts and the ballfield and the beach are empty. Back home yesterday, I dusted and oiled the stationary exercise bicycle, and turned the odometer back to zero.

This new season, I will pedal two miles a day five days a week in the basement until I reach San Francisco or summer returns, whichever happens first. Last year, I dropped out before Christmas, somewhere east of Chicago. I will make it this year, starting out just as soon as the hole in my toe, my last sweet souvenir of summer, is gone.

FALL

Well-meaning people often ask sportswriters, even middle-aged sportswriters, what they are going to do when they grow up. The sports department of a newspaper is sometimes called "the toy department," and whenever a sportswriter seems to be getting a little serious, someone will take him aside and say "Take it easy, friend, it's only fun and games."

Anyone who would say that is no friend and probably not too smart either. Sports is certainly not fun and games to a halfback facing knee surgery or a gasping runner trying to break four minutes for the mile or a sportswriter who wants to cover a beat with the same intelligence and professionalism that mark the other sections of a responsible newspaper.

Politics, race, religion, money, the law—all play roles in sports. If anyone had ever doubted this, the 1968 Olympics, the so-called problem Games, proved to the world that sports is no sanctuary from reality.

I

Joe Namath
Is a Student of the Game

Joe Namath hunches wolfishly out of the sauna, pads across the near-empty dressing room, and roots in the thicket of fan letters, play books, film cans, and scouting reports on the top shelf of his open wooden locker. He pulls out a gift-wrapped box.

He opens the box with great interest and unfolds a pair of white cotton drawers upon which a stranger has lovingly sewn the name and insignia of the New York Jets. Namath is pleased, touched by the time and effort, but disappointed: The drawers are several sizes too wide. Someone had thought he was larger than life.

Namath shrugs, gives the drawers to the dressing-room attendant, and continues our conversation. He had said recently that most spectators don't really know what is happening at a football game. On this fall day in 1967, as he dresses after a practice session, he reconsiders his remark and decides he was right in the first place.

"I throw a pass that's intercepted," says Namath, sipping at a can of soda, "and people blame me when it was the fault of someone who wasn't where he should have been. I throw a touchdown pass, and I get the credit when it was badly thrown and only a great catch made the play."

Namath shrugs and says he is not complaining. After all, he doesn't understand nuclear physics. Today's football is getting more complex by the minute. By the time he was in high school, he says, he realized that very few people could actually follow what he was talking about.

"I can explain things to people with diagrams," he says. "Sometimes in nightclubs I'll borrow a waiter's pencil and draw it all out if it's something that's bothering me and I want to explain. But most of the time I try not to get into it too much because people just don't understand."

Namath takes down a play book and flips through it. "It's getting more and more technical every day. A defensive player might not understand something an offensive player would understand. I think most fans grasp the basics well enough, but they don't have access to the plays and films we do, and if they did, who would expect them to study as hard as we do?"

Big linemen, their faces chafed from the cold, begin straggling into the locker room after breaking into a sweat on the field. Showers hiss. A young man at the far end of the dressing room is pushing a slim booklet onto the top shelf of each locker.

"I get this a lot," says Namath, pulling on gold corduroy slacks, slipping bare feet into matching suede shoes. "A receiver is wide open, and people want to know why I didn't throw to him. Well, I've held the ball for four seconds now, and a defensive man leaves, and it looks as though there's a receiver free. But it's too late. I don't have the time anymore to go back and turn and throw to him.

"Emerson Boozer made a great run a few weeks ago, and everybody talked about it. But what about the four blocks along the way? A kicker misses, but was it his fault or the holder's, or maybe the snap from center was bad?"

The young man is about to slip a booklet onto Namath's shelf, but the quarterback sees it is from the Fellowship of Christian Athletes and shakes his head. "I won't have a chance to read it," he says.

The young man moves on, saying nothing, and Namath calls after him, "Well, I got to be honest. There's no point wasting them. They're fine things, but I just won't have the time."

II

Tips from a Man
Who Eats to Win

We were sitting in a restaurant called The Elegant Farmer, in Oakland, California, and Bozo Miller, the world's champion eater, said, "The secret in my game is speed. I'm not as good as I used to be—who is?—but to beat me you almost have to kill me."

He downed his whiskey neat, and, from behind thick spectacles, morosely regarded his empty glass. He swung his arm overhead as if waving in an airplane. When the waitress finally arrived, Bozo said, "You're not watching me, honey. You better start bringing them three at a time."

Bozo shrugged, an enormous gesture, and continued. "Now, some of these pro-football players think they're pretty good eaters. Some gamblers are trying to match me up with one of the Buffalo players, a fellow with good size. Height means nothing. I'm only about five-foot seven, down to two-seventy-five, maybe two-eighty right now, but that's a good proportion. You get one of these ballplayers, six-seven or six-eight, even one who weighs close to three hundred pounds, he doesn't have a properly stretched stomach."

The waitress returned with the drinks, and Bozo jabbed a fat forefinger at me. "My friend here is getting hungry, honey. How about eight club sandwiches?"

The waitress was new, and she blinked twice before she understood.

"Even if one of those ballplayers could handle, say, a few three-pound steaks, I'd switch to ice-cream sundaes on my turn. No athlete could handle something that rich, and if he could, I'd destroy him with hot sauces or minestrone soup. Fluids is one of my strengths."

Bozo told me he was born Edwin Abraham Miller in 1908 in San Francisco. He realized early in life that he had "a good capacity," probably inherited from his father, a circus clown and nightclub comedian, who died young of diabetes. Young Bozo would eat forty hot dogs during a nine-inning baseball game just to amuse his friends. He drifted to New York, where he worked for bookmakers and hung out with a race-track crowd that even through the Depression had money to pay his feed bills. Mark Hellinger and Damon Runyon, two famous newspapermen of the era, would put Bozo up to such stunts as eating a small French restaurant out of all its desserts, and then they would write about it.

"That's for fun, to shake people up and give them a laugh," said Bozo. But, he said, there is no enjoyment in eating when big money rides on every bite. Bozo's most important match is said to have taken place in 1963 in the back room of a San Francisco restaurant called Trader Vic's. Bozo won the coin toss, elected chicken for easy tearing, and gulped down twenty-seven 2-pound pullets. After a while, his challenger, a Los Angeles man, licked off his fingers, sat back, and just watched his ten thousand dollars being gobbled up.

Bozo said he had trained for two weeks for that match, forcing down food and fluids to the bursting point each day, gaining more than twenty-five pounds, and stretching his stomach properly.

The sandwiches arrived with three more drinks, and Bozo began to eat, very efficiently and very neatly. "Besides having self-confidence and the know-how to pick the right foods, I have fast reflexes and good coordination. Speed is all-important. Get it down fast, you destroy your opponent. Speed is more important than endurance in this game. Slow and steady is for turtles and hares. Once I had twenty-five Seven-Ups down before my opponent had eight. He got discouraged. He said, 'You're crazy,' and he walked out."

Bozo leaned across the table. "You're not eating."

Bozo's talents brought him valuable publicity in his liquor business and made him a sought-after guest at bars and restaurants in northern California. The rare nights he stayed home, he cooked gourmet dinners, which his wife and teen-aged daughters helped him serve. He claimed that no one but himself had ever been able to finish one of his meals.

He finished six of the club sandwiches and impatiently motioned me to eat up and drink down. "Let's get this stuff out of the way," said Bozo. "We've got to figure out what we want for dinner."

III

The 1968 Olympics: The Reds and the Blacks and the Gold

In a telephone conversation one day, the president of the International Olympic Committee, Avery Brundage, said: "If we stop the Games every time there is disorder in the world, there would never be Games. At least there is one place in this troubled world free from politics, from religion, from racial prejudice . . ."

The Leader

Harry Edwards, tall and Black and hard, sat on the edge of a New York hotel bed. "If there is a religion in this country," he said, "it is athletics. On Saturdays from one to six you know where you can find a substantial portion of the country—in the stadium or in front of the television set. We want to get to those people, to affect them, to wake them up to what's happening in this country because otherwise they won't care."

Edwards was twenty-five years old at the time, a sociology instructor at San Jose State, a 6-foot 8-inch former discus thrower and basketball player. He had caused a national stir early in the 1967 football season when he led a protest against the housing available for Black athletes. Many Black football players, he had charged, were forced to live in motels miles from the school when there was vacant housing near the campus—but for whites only. His protest had led to the cancellation of a football game. Then he had caused an international stir with the formation of a group called the Olympic Committee for Human Rights.

"We're not just talking about boycotting the 1968 Olympics," Edwards said that night in his hotel room. "We're talking about the survival of society. What value is it to a Black man to win a medal if he returns to be relegated to the hell of Harlem? And what does society gain by some Negro winning a medal while other Negroes back home are burning down the country?"

Edwards watched a plastic-tipped cigar grow cold. "I think the time is gone when the Black man is going to run and jump when the white man says so, and then come back home to run and jump some more to keep from being lynched."

Bike Racer

"It starts as a game," said Jack Simes, Jr., "and then it gets to be a Frankenstein."

Jack Simes, Jr., would know. His eighty-year-old father bore scars on his head from bicycle-racing accidents, and Jack could vividly remember ending his own career in 1947 in a bloody tangle on a San Francisco track. Now we were sitting in the grandstand of a bike track in Kissena Park,

Queens, New York, watching the third generation of cycling Simeses loosen up for the 1964 national championships, a major step toward Olympic qualification.

"The trouble with coaching your own son," said Jack Simes, Jr., who was fifty, "is fear. For Jackie, the butterflies end when the race starts. For me, they just begin. I know what can happen to him."

He leaned forward, his eyes moving over the quarter-mile asphalt track until he picked out his son, a small, compactly built twenty-one-year-old with reddish-blond hair, crouched over the handlebars of a custom-built bike.

"His mother can't watch him anymore, she gets sick to her stomach," said Jack Simes, Jr. "Sprinting, you fall off a bike and it's like falling out of an automobile going fifty miles an hour."

Jack Simes III had broken his shoulder three times and smashed his nose. His legs were marked by old scars. Two years before, in Copenhagen, he had fractured his skull. He had been offered professional contracts in Europe, where a top sprint-cyclist can earn as much as fifty thousand dollars a year. But he had decided to remain an amateur and compete in the Olympics.

"The boy is always thinking," said Jack Simes, Jr., tense as his son jockeyed for position on his frail, 15-pound bike, letting the pacesetter break the wind for him.

"It's about fifty percent tactics, fifty percent muscle. You have to know your opponents' weaknesses, their strong points. Can you afford to let him get ahead to break the wind? Will you be able to catch up? What about his jump?"

Simes leaned forward as the riders edged into the curve, measured their opponents, then jumped—that moment when the rider stands in the saddle and explodes into final speed. As they hit the stretch, young Simes was fourth.

"Never make it now, not quite," muttered the father, trying not to look at the track. But his eyes kept flicking back as his son's thighs bunched, his back strained, his wrists grew thick from effort.

Suddenly young Simes swept past the field, stood up like a jockey, leaned forward, and slowed down by putting a gloved hand on the exposed front wheel.

Simes sighed and turned to me, grinning. "My daughter wanted to be a bike racer too, but I blew the whistle on that, I sure did."

Kalamazoo

Steve Mokone, the first Black African to play major league soccer in England, was born in Johannesburg, the son of a cab driver. He remembers playing a great deal of soccer, barefoot—first kicking bound rags, then a worn tennis ball. He sat in a wooden chair one day and remembered, with some reluctance, the feeling of his South African youth.

"I remember most," he said softly, "the pettiness and the insults and the brutal kinds of feelings you have when someone throws ink on your new white shirt, or punches you off the sidewalk, or walks off without paying you for caddying eighteen holes of golf. Or a policeman shoves cigarette butts up your nose and there is nothing you can do about it. There is no recourse because you are Black."

When Mokone was fourteen years old, his family moved to Pretoria. He became a star of the Sunday Black leagues and a matriculated college student. The full force of South Africa's repressive control had not yet dropped upon the nonwhites, and many of them still lived in the major cities. So it was possible, by an accident, for Mokone to break free.

One Saturday, while sight-seeing, the coach of a touring British team, Wolverhampton, saw Mokone working out. They talked. The coach returned on Sunday to watch Mokone play and offered him a professional contract.

Mokone's mother insisted that he continue school. But British correspondents touring with the Wolverhampton team filed such long and glorious dispatches about the barefoot discovery that many other offers followed. A year later, at eighteen, Mokone went to Coventry, England, lured by the promise of more playing time and experience with a third-division club. It was a mistake, he says now; he should have accepted a contract with a better club. But it eventually worked out. He was very popular, a great novelty in England, although the first few months were very difficult. He had to learn to play in soccer shoes and to overcome his fear of bodily contact with white men.

"There was a lot to learn," said Mokone. "One day my landlady rushed in, excited. She said she had found me a 'homeboy.' It turned out he was from Ghana, and she couldn't understand why we didn't know each other.

"I had a friend who always got into fights when we went to the pubs. He was Irish, and he told me he was getting back at the Englishmen who had discriminated against his people. And I had thought white men discriminated only against Black men."

In 1958, after three seasons, Mokone made his first trip home. It was very hard now to hear white men refer to his mother as a "jane," to slip back into the accommodating postures, to be a boy after having been a man. Although he was a great hero among Black South Africans, who all knew that he had been bought by the first-division team in Amsterdam, The Netherlands, and that he was nicknamed Kalamazoo after a song of that time, he was still unknown among white South Africans.

His success, said Mokone, looking back, was a threat to the concept of white supremacy. During his trip home he had been routinely arrested on pass violations and roughed up. Mokone went on to play for clubs in Cardiff, Wales; Marseilles, France; and Turin, Italy; but he returned to South Africa only once more, in 1962. Two years later he ended his career, and in 1965, he came to the United States to complete his education.

When I met him, he was a thirty-year-old student at the University of Rochester, with a wife and a small daughter, and the beginnings of a paunch even his vest could not hide. He was in New York, speaking to anyone who would listen about the hypocrisy of allowing South Africa to participate in the 1968 Olympic Games.

"I cannot understand why they give this kind of preferential treatment to South Africa, to allow her to break the Olympic Constitution," said Mokone. "The Black man will not be allowed to participate in fair trials with the whites for places on the team. There is great athletic talent in the Black townships, but the white man will never see it."

The Swordsman

"The true saber fencer," sneered an old épée man at the Olympic trials, "spends at least one year in acting school." As if on cue, the national saber champion, Jack Keane, screamed, wrenched up his mask, and whipped his blade against the copper fencing strip as his eyes rolled toward the ceiling of the gym. "Nice, but a minor performance," said the old épée man coolly. "You should see his crucifixion scene. Superb."

Keane, a dark and mercurial man, lost the bout in an upset and stalked to a corner, a titan nibbled to death by geese. "I am a sophisticated fencer," he said through closed teeth, "and I am being judged by men too inexperienced to see my subtle moves—zap, zap, zap—to the wrist. Three times, and they never saw it."

Keane glowered burningly, since all saber men must constantly try to intimidate the officials, intimidate each other, intimidate the fates that will eventually clog their synapses and turn their legs to lead. While foil fencers and épée fencers are electrically judged by flashing lights and buzzers, the saber fencer is judged by men—whose eyes may be slower than his blade.

Saber fencing is not as easy to follow as the clear, straight thrusting of the épée or the controlled flurries of the foil. The saber is a bold weapon, descended from the cavalry sword, and a touch can be scored by slashing or banging or sticking or slicing to any part of the head or upper body. Saber fencing can become very emotional and saber fencers tend to posture like bullfighters and tenors.

The tension was obvious on the day of the Olympic trials in Teaneck, New Jersey. The saber fencers came into the tournament with points accrued from regional and national competitions throughout the year, but a poor showing could keep even a star like Keane off the team.

"I feel horrible, miserable, *aaaargh,*" Keane had said early in the morning, flashing his great white smile, tossing his crisp black curls. As creative director on the Nixon-for-President advertising account, Keane had had little time to rest or practice recently, he said.

It was going to be a very hard day for Keane. First, as often happens in fencing matches, the four judges helping the bout director were other fencers either waiting their turns or already eliminated. Whether or not some of them were too inexperienced to see Keane's "subtle moves," they were all suspected of being secretly hostile: Saber men, not always without justification, are paranoid. By the final round, the fencers, acting in rare concert, were boycotting certain officials.

Second, Keane's bounding style—his saber held arrogantly low as he peacocks along the strip—nearly impaled him on a spike left carelessly sticking out of a wooden post in the small Fairleigh Dickinson University gym. As he twisted and jerked in agony, clutching his spine, spectators covered their eyes and other fencers raised their eyebrows.

Third, Keane was tired. His strength has always been in his determination and fierce combativeness. While other fencers may vary the tempo of their game to press and relax alternately, Keane never lets up. But this day he was wearing down, and the tight skin around his jaw had begun to sag. He looked his forty years.

But Keane hung in grimly, shrieking, and who was to say that his intimidations didn't help? One young judge cried, "It was good, it was good, Jack, believe me, I heard it hit you." And Alex Orban, the great instinctive fencer, snarled at the judge, "Be positive."

"I just want to make the team," Keane kept saying, and naturally he ended the regular final round in a tie for first place with Orban, who is ten years younger. Keane lost, and flashed his dazzling smile and tossed his now soggy curls and congratulated everyone who, like him, was going to Mexico City, stopping only now and then to touch his spine or grit his teeth or check to see if his heart was still beating.

The old épée man, disinterested, nodded his head at me. "I'll tell you all you need to know about fencers," he said.

"When General Maxwell Taylor discontinued varsity fencing at West Point, a delegation of fencers from the New York area went up to complain. After all, the sword is a military weapon. Maxwell Taylor looked at them and said, 'Frankly, gentlemen, it's the cost.'

"Well, everyone laughed. After all, what was six thousand or so dollars a year to the army? So Maxwell Taylor said, 'Frankly, gentlemen, it's the lack of facilities.'

"Well, everyone laughed. After all, West Point had the best fencing room in the country. It had been built into the original structure. So finally Maxwell Taylor said, "Gentlemen, fencing is a sport for intellectuals, and we don't want intellectuals in the army.' "

The Party Line

A year earlier, in Moscow, a Soviet sports official had told me, "When we see Leonid Zhabotinsky break another weight-lifting record we do not say 'Aha, a clear-cut victory over capitalism.' That is foolish. It is not sport. But we must realize that his feat cannot exist outside of space and time, and it is the product of a particular society with a particular culture.

"There must be some interrelation between Zhabotinsky's feat and the advantages of a socialistic system that gives possibilities to workers, students, and peasants to practice sport and go to the Olympic Games."

* * * *

Parade

And it finally came to pass. On a cloudy, mild Saturday in October, a tall and tawny Mexican hurdler moved lithely up ninety carpeted steps to the rim of a rock-hewn stadium, turned slowly to present her torch to the world, then plunged it into a stainless steel saucer and fired the flame that would burn through the Games of the nineteenth Olympiad.

There were about one hundred thousand of us in the Olympic stadium. Most were upper-class Mexicans who could afford the expensive tickets. Many were tourists and journalists who had started their day early to reach the great new stadium that seemed to flow from the gray stone as if it had been roughly scooped out by the hand of a god.

We had come from the heart of the city in buses and cars, along handsome, sweeping freeways that knifed through green belts and through adobe shanty towns that had been hastily, pathetically, splashed with white and red and pink and blue paint for the Games.

I remember staring through the tinted windows of the bus at dark Indian faces watching without expression. Donkeys and ragged dogs scrounged by the roadside, where small children and women with babies swaddled to their breasts picked their way among piles of refuse and stone. A man stood, balanced on a home-made wooden leg, in the cindery courtyard of his shack, distractedly kicking at a soccer ball.

Now, inside the stadium, Avery Brundage, eighty-one

years old, was reading a speech in Spanish. The beautiful legions of the world were massed about him: Senegalese so black their skin seemed blue and Swedes with cornsilk hair; well-dressed throngs from the United States and the Soviet Union and Japan and Germany; and four men, in suits that did not match, from poor, corrupt little Haiti. The crowd was especially warm toward the contingent from Czecho-slovakia, for that country had just been overrun by Soviet tanks. And the pride and joy in the Mexican marchers seemed to contrast oddly with the underground news photos we had seen of the Mexican student protesters who had been machine-gunned in the streets only a few weeks before.

The ceremony was very beautiful and moving, doves whirling into the air and the symbolic passing of flags. Brundage stood ramrod straight. There were no South Africans in the Olympics—he had compromised on that—but here we all were, 7,350 feet above the level of the sea, watching a flame fed by gas burn evenly against a pale-blue sky.

Volleyball

The first day of competition was a tough one for the American women's volleyball team. They ate early—a large breakfast because their team manager, Dr. Marie Liba, insisted upon it—and then straggled out into the bright sunshine that gleamed off the windows and bricks of Olympic Village. The thirteen of them were living in five small rooms, with three bathrooms. It was Sunday, and six of them attended early Catholic Mass. The usual morning crush in the bathrooms was lessened. It was the best thing that happened all day.

The women, most of them lanky blondes in their twenties, were quiet on the bus trip out to the Olympic gymnasium, leafing through the color spreads in the Mexican newspapers, of the previous day's opening ceremony. Several complained mildly and routinely about the inadequate laundry room, about the lack of a place to dance at the Village, and about how hard they worked for their coach, Harlan Cohen. A 2-mile run in under sixteen minutes every day, one hundred sit-ups—imagine! Volleyball is getting to be a young girl's game, they said.

I was sitting next to Barbara Perry, a tall, dark, jolly athlete from Honolulu. "It's really rough playing the Japanese right off," she said. "We don't expect to win, just be respectable. What makes it tough is that we play Czechoslovakia tomorrow, and we might beat them if we have some rest and confidence."

Coach Cohen, a tough little bachelor schoolteacher from Los Angeles, herded the women into a warm-up room off the main arena as soon as we reached the gym. I found myself talking with Dr. Liba. "We've got good girls," she said; "they don't smoke or drink, no discipline problems. Of course, I've insisted we all live together, so no one can sneak in after the ten o'clock curfew. Not that they would, anyway. Tomorrow night—after Czechoslovakia—I'll let them stay out until midnight."

101

The match between the Americans and Japanese began with all the music and marches and exchanges of gifts that make international competition so ceremonial and entertaining. All the Japanese players were taller than the average Japanese woman, but considerably smaller than the American players. They had been formed into a team six years before by a legendary fanatical coach named Hirofumi Diamatsu, who had them all working at one factory, living together, spending all their free hours on the hardwood floors. The crowd cheered the Japanese and casually booed the Americans. I asked an Olympic press aide, an Argentine, if the booing was part of the anti-American feeling we had noticed during the opening parade. He said No, it was just the crowd letting the Americans know that it had already seen them play.

The match lasted fifty-two minutes, and the scores were 15–6, 15–2, 15–2. Women's volleyball is usually a highly emotional game. There is a great deal of screaming and hand-clapping and shouted instructions as the players tumble and slide and jump. But the Americans lost their zip early —it was very hard to keep spiking when a solid wall of orange uniforms kept rising up to bat the ball back into their faces. And it was very hard to keep diving for balls that the Japanese scientifically slammed just a few inches from outstretched American fingers.

The Japanese volleyball team is one of the true and pure joys of modern sport, a team of six bodies so well trained that head or chest or stomach can return a ball as well as closed fist. The Japanese women's breasts were bound with elastic, to give them greater mobility. Yet there was nothing mechanical about the spring in their legs or the quick chatter in the back court or the joyful squeals when they won.

The bus back to Olympic Village was even quieter. Coach Cohen said his team had never played so well, and he thought they'd do better when they became more accustomed to playing together.

"This is nothing," said Barbara Perry. "There'll be real pressure later on when we play teams we think we have a chance to beat."

The Vietnamese

"Our biggest problem is morale," said Phan Nhu My with a sad smile. "We must constantly repeat the Olympic slogan to the team: It is more important to compete than to win. We remind them how much more fortunate they are than thousands of Vietnamese back home. Sometimes it helps."

The two cyclists on the Republic of South Vietnam team came to Mexico City with virtually no special training for the high altitude there. The two girl swimmers trained in Paris, Tokyo, and Singapore on their fathers' money. The entrant in the decathlon preferred to work out when no one was around to laugh at him. The fencer was eliminated early— as most Vietnamese athletes have been since 1952, the first and last time they came as a national team representing the North and South.

103

"We do not have a great tradition in sports," admitted My, editor of the Vietnam Press Agency, secretary of his country's Olympic committee and chief of its mission at the Games. "When the French came to our country, they imported the European sports—cycling, tennis, football, rowing. We have a little wrestling art of our own, and some boxing, like Thai boxing. We allow kicking, bare knuckles, and elbowing."

We were sitting in a small interview room in the administration building of Olympic Village. My was chain-smoking. "The president and the prime minister agreed that we have to be here," he said, "to show the world that even a country at war is trying to normalize its life."

With their presence planned as a political gesture, the Vietnamese had begun preparing for the 1968 Olympics only in mid-1967. The government allocated five million piasters (about $42,500) for the team. Selection was not difficult: Virtually all Vietnamese athletes were either in American universities or living in Saigon.

Of the ten-member team, the three shooters were Saigon policemen, the two track-and-field men were students at San Fernando Valley State College in California, and the fencer, an army major, had recently returned from Texas State. The two girls—daughters of a doctor and a ship-owner—had learned to swim in the 30-meter pool of the exclusive Cercle Sportif Saigonnais; to prepare for competition at the 50-meter Olympic distance, the girls had been sent abroad.

Of the two cyclists, one was a soldier, the other a seventeen-year-old boy soon to be conscripted, according to My. Once quite popular, competition cycling has never been the same since the Tour de Vietnam was cancelled in 1963 when the government could no longer assure security on the roads.

South Vietnam has won a few medals in the Southeast Asia Games from time to time, particularly with its fine teams in volleyball, table tennis, and soccer, the national sport. But despite coaching and equipment from the American military, sports training remains out of reach for most Vietnamese. There is, for example, a well-equipped rowing organization, but the wealthy Vietnamese businessmen who belong to the club row only for pleasure and have no interest in training young oarsmen or scullers.

Preparation for the Olympics was halted for five months by the Tet offensive of January, 1968, and then the allocation was cut in half. Phan Nhu My said that even with the five million piasters originally promised there had been no thought of bringing more athletes or even of better training for the ones they had. The additional money would have gone for "public relations."

"In my room at the Village," he said, "are many books and pamphlets and souvenirs from other countries, telling their stories. If we had more money, we would have printed many such books, and we would have given receptions and offered entertainments."

The Vietnamese sportsmen had been apprehensive about coming to Mexico, a country they knew only from American western movies. But they were delighted by the ovation they received when they marched into the Olympic stadium on opening day, and they were charmed by the sympathy and kindness of the Mexicans.

Patiently they explained to the Mexicans that they were from the south of their country, and that only the 1952 team had represented the entire country. To his relief, said Phan Nhu My, the Mexicans seemed to show no particular favoritism toward either South or North Vietnam.

Another bright spot, according to My, has been the continuing friendship of other Asian countries. The day before My and I met, the Filipinos, Thais, Koreans, Malaysians, and Vietnamese formed a mutual defense pact for the 196-kilometer road race. It was felt that an Asian cycling alliance was necessary to offset the traditional agreements among the European racers.

The greatest frustration, My said, was trying to overcome the "inferiority complexes" of the athletes. After lengthy "negotiations," the coach persuaded the decathlon man to train with athletes from other countries. But then he insisted upon placing the pole vault bar considerably higher than the 11½ feet which was his limit.

The athlete explained that he would be humiliated if the other athletes knew that he could vault no higher than 11½ feet. He would rather keep knocking the bar off, giving the impression he was just having a bad day.

"We made him to understand," said My, "that we are not here to win, or even do well, but to learn and give our most. Then if the situation comes to a normal state, if peace should come at the end of this year or next year, we will be ready to make rapid progress in sports and take our place among the other nations of Asia."

Black Power

In the evening of the fourth day of competition, Tommie Smith and John Carlos lowered their heads and raised their black-gloved fists as "The Star-Spangled Banner" was played to celebrate Smith's victory in the 200-meter race. I thought at the time it was a pretty mild gesture for two Black athletes who were students at San Jose State, Harry Edwards' school.

Winners

Jack Simes III, the third generation of cycling Simeses, did not win a medal in the 1968 Olympics. Nor did Jack Keane, the histrionic saber fencer. There were no medals for the hammer-throwing rivals, Harold Connolly and Ed Burke; and Klim, the Soviet athlete that Burke wanted to beat, was beaten himself and finished second. There were no medals for the Vietnamese or for the American women's volleyball team, or, for that matter, for most of the thousands of athletes who came to Mexico City. And for most of them, returning home without medals was not a crushing disappointment—having been there, having competed against the best in the world, was medal enough.

107

* * * *

View from the Top

"From the standpoint of our image in the world, our way of life, the Olympics was a success," said Douglas F. Roby, the president of the United States Olympic Committee.

We were talking on the telephone. I asked him about the United States Olympic Committee's suspension of Smith and Carlos after they had raised their fists and lowered their heads. The two athletes were thrown off the team and made to leave the Olympic Village.

"We suppressed the demonstrators," said Roby, "because we felt if we let it go, it would get progressively worse, it would become a tip-off to others, white as well as Black. We let a lot of little things go by—berets, black socks, hands up and down—even though there are specific rules against changes in uniform in the competitor's handbook. But we felt that would be flyspecking.

"But we couldn't let a flagrant demonstration go by. We considered that we might have a boycott on our hands, but we had to take the chance."

The following day, according to Roby, he wanted to be sure that all athletes knew of the committee's decision, so he approached Lee Evans, Larry James, and Ron Freeman as the three Black athletes were preparing for the 400-meter run.

"Now, boys," he said he told them, "I don't want to upset you, but . . ."

In stony silence the three listened to Roby warn them that "any further demonstration would be dealt with to the full extent of the United States Olympic Committee's powers." Then they went out and swept the event, finishing one, two, and three and arriving at the victory stand in black socks and black berets. They raised their fists in the Black Power gesture.

"My talk spurred them on," chuckled Roby. He added that the berets were acceptable because it was raining and because they removed them during the anthem. The raised, clenched fists were lowered during the anthem. Besides, said Roby, the raised fist was just a traditional athletic gesture of triumph that he remembered from his own playing days at the University of Michigan and with Cleveland in the National Football League.

Roby was seventy, the retired board chairman of a Detroit company that manufactured automobile parts. He said that the two problems he faced during the 1968 Olympics—the generation gap and the Black-white confrontation—would be ameliorated with time. When today's young people get to be "thirty or thirty-five, they'll look back and see how foolish they were," he added.

He was rather disturbed, however, by the behavior of the all-white Harvard heavyweight crew. After they were selected to represent the United States in the Olympics, six of the nine crew members issued a statement supporting Harry Edwards' Olympic Project for Human Rights.

Later the rowers circulated a letter asking other white

athletes to consider the inequality in America and the possibility of using the Games as a stage for nonviolent protest.

On the telephone that day, Robby said "they defied us" by "embarking on a social justice and civil-rights program" instead of concentrating on their rowing, "especially after we had spent fourteen thousand dollars to ship their shells and equipment down to Mexico."

I asked him if he was glad that the Harvard crew had lost.

"I won't say I'm glad they lost," said Roby. "I was terribly disappointed. But it verified my feeling that you can't head out on one project and expect to do well in another."

Aftermath

"The Games were a success," said Harry Edwards, "because the demonstration proved to all athletes that there's more to being a nigger than the color of a man's skin. If Smith and Carlos could be treated like that by Olympic officials, so could any athlete.

"Yes, I'd say it was a very successful Olympics. A foundation was laid for athletes and fans to become more involved. It was all nonviolent, no fire-bombing, and no one got stomped.

"Were there historic milestones? I don't know, but we turned over some rocks and saw what was underneath."

110

WINTER

Writing under deadline is often exhilarating, and if you're lucky and the event has moved you, a rhythm develops and the story just flows out of the typewriter. This happens in boxing, in tennis, in auto, horse, and crew racing more than in most sports because the action is centralized and fairly simple. Football, baseball, and basketball are more difficult because along with most of the same deadline pressures come the complicated statistics and constant player substitutions.

I never wrote so many stories so fast as during the four years that boxing was my beat. A fight might be over at 11:15 P.M. on a night when all the copy had to be in the Times' office by 11:30 if it was to make the next morning's paper. Actually this was easier than it sounds. After I typed each paragraph, I would tear it out of the typewriter and hand it to the Western Union telegrapher sitting next to me at ringside, who would punch it out over a direct line to a similar machine and operator in the Times' sports department office. This worked whether I was just seven blocks away in the old Madison Square Garden or in the Astrodome in Houston, Texas.

Getting the story to the office is sometimes more difficult than gathering the facts or shaping them into a coherent piece. But with modern communication systems, the problem is usually just a matter of time. At night in a chilly arena, with the clock moving toward the deadline, that moment comes when even the best story in the world, finished too late, is worthless.

I

Tiger

Dick Tiger was the middleweight champion of the world when I first met him. He looked almost comical that day, moving down Eighth Avenue in New York on the balls of his feet like a big black cat, a homburg perched on the top of his head.

The homburg was too small for him, but it was years before I learned that he always bought his hats a size too small so he could share them with his brothers back home in Nigeria.

As we walked down Eighth Avenue, his manager was saying, "African fighters are very good, very tough. They're closer to the jungle."

"There is no jungle in Nigeria," said Tiger without smiling.

"It's just an expression, Dick, just a figure of speech," said the manager hastily. "I mean they're hungry fighters."

Tiger bounced on down Seventeenth Street and up three flights of stairs in the Catholic Youth Organization building. We followed him through a clean, brightly lit gym and into the dressing room.

As the homburg, the light-brown sports jacket, the white shirt, and the blue tie disappeared into a rusty metal locker,

Tiger seemed to grow larger, to shed the comedy of his clothes. The blue tribal tattoos across his chest and back rippled over knotty muscle and made him seem suddenly savage.

But there was only gentleness in his eyes, and humor twitched at the corners of his mouth. I watched him tape his hands with great care, slowly, first winding the bandages around and around, then placing the sponge across the knuckles, then wrapping on the adhesive. Very few champions tape their own hands, and I asked him why he didn't have his manager or trainer take care of this daily chore.

"I am a traveling man, and I got to do things myself. A fighter should know these things," he said. "This is my business."

It had been his business for eleven years then, since he had become a professional fighter at the age of twenty-three. He told me that he was born in Amaigbo, a remote eastern Nigerian town in the rain forests of the Binin River Delta. He was raised on a farm and educated at an Anglican mission school, where classes were held in his tribal language, Ibo, as well as in English. At nineteen he went to the city of Aba to work in his brother's grocery store. At a local boys' club he learned to box.

He had been christened Richard Ihetu—Ibo for "what I want"—but when he began fighting professionally he took the ring name Dick Tiger. His opponents included Easy Dynamite, Black Power, and Mighty Joe Young. He beat them all and attracted the attention of British boxing promoters. But lonely and cold in the dank gyms of London and

114

Liverpool, he lost his first four fights in Britain.

Letters from his family in Nigeria were beseeching him to give up the foolishness and return to his father's farm or his brother's grocery store. Tiger gave himself one more chance. In his fifth fight, he knocked out a Liverpool boy in ninety seconds, and Richard Ihetu, farmer and clerk, was gone forever.

"That was it, man. Oh, that was it," he said nostalgically, years later, as he finished taping his hands for the afternoon's workout.

Dick Tiger worked harder in the gym than any other fighter I have ever seen. He believed that the foundation of his success was good physical condition. He could hit hard but so could many middleweights; his boxing skills improved each year, but he always lacked finesse. But Dick Tiger had never been knocked down, and no fighter had ever tired him out in the ring. Dick Tiger would stand and fight all day if necessary and let his opponent wear himself out.

"Whenever I'm tired," Tiger once told me, "I know my opponent is tired too. He's used up his strength just trying to hit me."

"That Tiger, he works like a horse, a real workhorse he is," said Jimmy August, the fat little trainer. "All business. He knows God built him like a horse, and he works like one. That right, Dick?"

"The gloves," said Tiger, holding out his taped hands. All business. There was no small talk for Tiger in the gym.

For two hours Tiger worked hard, ignoring the youngsters in the gym and the curious Catholic Youth Organization workers. Silver globules of sweat broke out on his forehead and ran together in streams down his body. Everything he did was methodical and intense, the rope slapping rhythmically under his feet, the light punching bag rattling twenty times at a clip against its wooden support, the heavy canvas-covered bag groaning and creaking at his left hooks, the floor of the gym complaining as the chunky 5-foot 8-inch fighter twisted his neck until his eyes popped and wrenched his torso and strained his legs and gave every blood vessel, bone, and muscle in his body a reason to jump out of its skin.

He had always worked hard. He was never a spectacular fighter or a controversial personality, so it took years for him to become established and get frequent fights. He first came to the United States in 1959 and lived in third-rate Manhattan hotels with his pregnant wife, cooking meals on a hot plate and running in nearby Central Park while he slowly gained the reputation among boxing people of an honest workman. His wife gave birth to twins and then to a third child in 1960. Tiger sent her back to Nigeria and began commuting between New York and Aba. He saved his money very carefully, walked whenever possible, and window-shopped for entertainment.

Late in 1962, he won the middleweight title from Gene Fullmer, and except that now he had more money to bring home to Abigail, his wife, very little changed. And he was still working harder than anyone else.

At the end of his two-hour workout, Tiger showered and dressed, shrinking back into his clothes, topping himself with his homburg. I did not think he looked comical any longer.

On our way out of the gym, a huge, red-faced policeman shook hands with Tiger and wished him luck.

"Are the constables in Nigeria as big as him?" asked Jimmy August, like a straight man feeding a line to a comedian.

"Sure," said Tiger, smiling, "'cause for breakfast they eat guys like him."

Everyone laughed, and Jimmy August poked me in the ribs. "Whatta sense of humor. Couple years ago, this reporter whose name I won't mention asked Dick if he was a cannibal, and Dick said, 'Not anymore, I quit after eating the governor-general and getting a bellyache.'"

We laughed some more and headed toward the subway at Eighth Avenue. Tiger said he felt very good, that he always felt good after a hard workout.

"This is my business," he said. "I work very hard at it now because it will not always be my business. I want to make money. I want six hundred thousand dollars. Now, all I have is a house and a Peugeot car, but I will have more houses and factories and shops."

He said that people in America did not realize how modern Nigeria was, that there were tall buildings in the capital, Lagos. People thought Nigeria was all jungle, he said, and filled with tigers.

"The only tiger I ever saw," he said, "was in a cage in the Liverpool Zoo."

* * * *

117

In the years that I covered boxing, I never met a fighter as single-minded, as even-tempered as Dick Tiger. When he lost his middleweight title at thirty-seven, and the experts wrote him off, he moved up in class to fight as a light-heavyweight. The morning after he won that championship, I found the same traveling philosopher. "The people all said that Tiger is finished, that he looks one hundred years old," he said, "and now they come around to pat my head and tell me I'm a good boy. That's life."

He went home to Nigeria with his championship money. When he returned in the spring of 1968, he was very upset. It was a different Tiger.

He sat in an overheated room in a cheap Manhattan hotel, his square hands opening and closing and plucking at his baggy gray pants, his voice rising, his mouth twisted. "I used to be a happy man," he said, "but now I have seen something I have never seen before. I read about killings and war, but I had never seen such things. Now I have seen massacres."

He bounded from the straight-backed chair and began fishing in his bureau drawers, through pamphlets and books and newspaper clippings. "Ah, here," he said, almost reverently opening some tissue paper. "This is Aba." He spread the photographs on the bed.

"The hospital. There were eight patients and a doctor when the planes came and threw bombs around. Hired pilots. The Nigerians can't fly planes. They are a thousand years behind civilization, that is why they are doing everything wrong.

118

"The open market, look at that. In that corner, that is a hand. A little girl's hand. What does she know of war? This woman burned. These men dead, not even soldiers. That is a woman too. No, it is not rags; it was a woman."

He carefully repacked the photographs and sat down again. "The Nigerian radio says Dick Tiger of Nigeria will defend his light-heavyweight championship. Dick Tiger of Nigeria. They still claim me, and they would kill me; they want to kill us all. I am a Biafran. I am Dick Tiger of Biafra. And we just want to live."

Tiger's view of the Nigeria-Biafra war was as straightforward as the pamphlets in his room. In 1966 thousands of Ibo tribesmen were slaughtered in pogroms in northern Nigeria. The Christian Ibos were civil servants and small businessmen in the Muslim north. The Ibos fled back to their eastern native lands and ultimately formed a new country, Biafra.

Under the slogan *To Keep Nigeria One,* federal troops attacked Biafra, murdering, looting, wasting, and starving their countrymen.

"Keep Nigeria one," spat Tiger derisively. "What will be left for them to rule if they keep killing our children?"

Tiger said he had moved his family, which now included seven children, from Aba, where he owned houses, cinemas, factories, and shops, to Amaigbo, the remote delta town of his birth. At thirty-eight, he had volunteered for the Biafran army, teaching physical fitness and acting as an inspiration. He gave no exhibitions because groups of soldiers dared not congregate for fear of strafing attacks.

119

"I do not worry so much anymore," said Tiger, restless on his wooden chair. "The children have learned to take cover quickly when they hear the bomber planes. It is the fighter planes we worry about. The bombs fall slowly. If you see them, you can run away. But you never see the bullets."

* * * *

He lost his light-heavyweight championship that year. He denied that thoughts of his family and of his country had weighed him down. He fought again after that, and won, but he was pushing forty now. His magnificent physical condition had carried him further than most fighters, but it could not carry him much longer.

Then one day before Christmas, 1969, we met in an office at Madison Square Garden. He needed help. In 1963, he explained, the British government had awarded him a medal, Member of the British Empire. When Tiger read that John Lennon, the Beatle, had returned his medal for reasons that included Great Britain's involvement in the Nigerian civil war, Tiger decided to mail back his medal, too. Would I help him draft the letter?

We wrote: *I am hereby returning the M.B.E. because every time I look at it, I think of millions of men, women and children who died and are still dying in Biafra because of the arms and ammunition the British Government is sending to*

Nigeria and its continued moral support of this genocide against the people of Biafra.

He signed it, Dick Tiger Ihetu.

We packed the medal, its pink ribbon now grimy, in a box addressed to the British Ambassador in Washington. Then we walked to the post office. As we walked up the steps in the brilliant, wintry afternoon, Tiger said: "If they ask me how much it's worth, what should I say?"

I shrugged. "We should try to pawn it and find out."

"I'll say a million dollars." Tiger laughed for the first time that day. "I'll say fifty or a hundred, just so it gets there."

He stood on line at the registry window, a small black hat perched on his head, his body muffled in a fur-lined coat.

The clerk behind the registry wicket hefted the package and shook his head. "No good, you got Scotch Tape on it. Go around the corner, they'll give you some brown paper."

Another line. Tiger has always been such a patient man, I thought, waiting for bouts, waiting for return bouts, waiting for his title shots, even now picking up fights where he can while waiting for one more title chance.

"If there had been no war," he said earlier that morning, "I would be retired by now. But . . . well . . ." He smiled and spread his hands. "I'm not getting rich or investing money. Now is just for daily bread and praying the war is over. I cannot complain. I am not the only one who lost property."

A clerk handed Tiger a long strip of gummed brown paper and a wet sponge in a dish. Tiger took it to a writing desk

121

and began to tear the brown paper into small strips, his thick fingers careful and precise. I watched and remembered him always taping his own hands.

He finished the package and showed it to me. "Well, now I know there is something else I can do."

There was another wait at the registry window. "If you look at Africa now," he said, "there is fighting and trouble in every country that once was under the British Government. They were forced to give the countries independence, but they gave it with the left hand and now are trying to take it back with the right hand."

He stopped suddenly. "I am not a politician. I don't want people to say, ah, there's a dumb fighter who does not speak good English talking."

"Okay," snapped the registry clerk, flipping the small package. "What's in it?"

"A medal," said Tiger softly.

"What?"

"A medal."

"What's it worth?"

Tiger shrugged. "I don't know. Fifty, hundred dollars?"

"No value," said the clerk, to himself. He weighed it, registered it, asked Tiger if he wanted it to go air mail. Tiger said yes.

"One sixty."

Tiger gave him two dollar bills and counted his change. He readjusted his scarf as he walked out into the bright street and smiled and shook my hand and could only say,

"Well . . ." and shrug and start down the steps.

I never saw Dick Tiger after that day. He fought several times, lost, and worked briefly as a guard at the Metropolitan Museum of Art, in New York. He found out he had cancer of the liver. He was penniless when he returned to Nigeria before Christmas, 1971, to die.

II

Jake the Snake
Is Hot on Ice

Jake the Snake loves his work. Three nights a week he crouches in front of a hockey goal, loose and agile on skinny steel blades, peering down the ice through the eye-slits of a plastic mask. He seems to say "I am Jacques Plante, the greatest goalie in the business, and I dare you to get one past me."

And of course they try, bursting through Plante's teammates, a swirl of color and flying ice roaring down toward the goal, thousands screaming as the stick cracks against a frozen rubber disk that gets smaller and harder as it hurtles at one hundred miles an hour toward Jacques Plante's throat.

Slap.

Time stands still, and thousands catch their breaths as Plante's big glove flicks out and kills the puck in its leather folds. Plante sinks to his knees, drawing out the last bit of emotional suspense. Then, as the breaths explode in a mighty *whoosh,* he disdainfully flips the puck away and watches the mad scramble start again.

"You must be born a goal tender, a man alone," said Plante one day over lunch. "Even the rule book says you are not a hockey player, that a team is made of five hockey players and a goal tender. You are a man who can prevent defeat, but you cannot win a game.

"The eyes are upon you. You are the target of the game. When a goal is scored, play stops and people talk. They say how you missed the puck, how you made a mistake. They do not talk of all the mistakes that were made before the opposing player took his shot. They say it is your mistake alone."

Across the table, Plante looked like a man born to accept such responsibility. He was thirty-four years old at the time, recently traded to New York, after nine seasons with Montreal. His face was strong and angular, with deep hollows beneath the scarred cheekbones and a quick mobility around the eyes and the mouth.

During a game, the face, which bears the marks of several hundred stitches, is covered with a 10-ounce, padded plastic mask. He introduced the mask to the National Hockey League in 1959 because, he admitted freely, he was tired of seeing his blood on the ice.

"During the game itself there is little time to be afraid. Once you are afraid in a game, you are through," he said in a clipped accent bearing traces of his native French.

"But I was not sleeping at night, replaying each game in my head—the pucks I stopped, and the ones that missed my head by an inch—thinking about more stitches and going back to the hospital. And wasn't four times enough for one nose to be broken?"

So he began wearing the mask in practice sessions. Then one night in New York, a Ranger backhanded a shot into the left side of Plante's nose. Jake the Snake went down.

The crowd waited impatiently for twenty minutes, while the game was held up so seven stitches could be taken on Plante's nose. When he skated out again, he was wearing his ghoulish Plexiglas mask.

A controversy began. Originally the Montreal coach said Plante might wear his mask only until his nose healed. But Plante refused to take it off. Fans called him a coward, but Plante was impervious to catcalls from the safe seats. Some hockey people felt the mask was unseemly and detrimental to a goalie's performance. Others thought it sensible and humane.

Montreal won its next eleven games. The mask stayed.

"I am the best goalie in the league," Plante said, "and with the mask I am even better. I can laugh at getting hit in the face. I can use my face to stop pucks."

A perennial winner of the best goalie award, Plante is widely imitated by youngsters throughout Canada. The mask soon became standard equipment, and Plante's innovative style of play was quickly copied. Unlike most goalies, who stay close to the net, Plante wanders—he moves around, plays the angles instead of the net, skates out to make saves and pass the puck, and shouts instructions at the defensemen.

For all his activity, agility, and grandstanding, Plante's biggest problem has always been breathing. He was raised in Shawinigan Falls, Quebec, and severe asthma kept him from competitive sports until he was in his teens. The son of a machinist, Jacques was the eldest of a large family, and he diapered, sewed, and cleaned for the brood.

Until he was fourteen years old, he slept sitting up, coughing all night, falling asleep at dawn when he was too tired to cough anymore. When he was fourteen, Jacques' condition improved, and he began playing hockey. He became winded too quickly to skate very long, so he played at goal.

The asthma has bothered him throughout his career, but he does not like to talk about it—although he admits that it must seem crazy for a man to leave his wife and children and such hobbies as oil painting and knitting to stand on ice and try to stop pucks.

"I worked very hard to get to the top, and now that I am here, I want to enjoy it, to taste it," he said.

"And there are those nights I go home, and I tell my wife I don't know how they could score. I filled the net tonight, I blocked it all, and every time they shot I scooped up the puck and laughed 'Aha, look what I found.' Nights like that keep me going, on nights like that I know I love what I do."

III

Dorold's Own
Starlet II Is a Fat Little Dog

A fat little pug named Dorold's Own Starlet II wiped her nose on Mrs. Elizabeth Keil's red jersey skirt.

"I think she's a little let down," said Mrs. Keil, dabbing at her own moist blue eyes. "Everybody's crazy about Starlet except the judges."

"Starlet's a nice little dog," I said to Mrs. Keil, and she brightened a little. We were sitting in a dim corner of the basement of Madison Square Garden. Upstairs, the annual Westminster Dog Show was in progress. Earlier in the day, Dorold's Own Starlet II had finished fourth in the open class for fawn bitches, but the rules forbade an owner from taking a dog home until the show was over, and so Mrs. Keil, a plump, pleasant, middle-aged woman, sat on a wooden chair in the basement and tried to keep smiling.

She was a widow, she said, and not a very good mixer, so she just watched the swirling crowd of people and animals. Slim, delicate young men snipped invisible hairs from the rumps of shaven poodles, and chilly, handsome booted blondes were towed through the aisles by lean, stalking whippets. A fat, small woman with a little green bow in her hair was tying an identical little green bow onto her Pekingese.

128

"I'm really not so disappointed," said Mrs. Keil, "because Starlet is only a pet—the only dog I have. It would be nice for her to win first place, but it's not so important."

Mrs. Keil said she lived alone in Kew Gardens, Queens, and had bought Starlet eighteen months earlier because she had heard that pugs were very affectionate and not particularly active. She had taken a bus to Englishtown, New Jersey, and had bought Starlet for two hundred dollars, from a recommended kennel. A woman friend had helped her lug the dog home on the bus.

A woman at the kennel rather pointedly told Mrs. Keil that she hoped all of Starlet's "good training wouldn't go to pot." The dog was ten months old at the time and had won a few ribbons at some small shows.

Mrs. Keil thought about that for a long time. She felt she did have a responsibility to Starlet's breeding and training, but it would be so difficult: She had no car, no children, not much extra money to spend on so expensive a hobby. When Mr. Keil was alive—he had died five years earlier—there was usually a dog around the house, but not for show.

Once, she remembered mistily, they had a little wire-haired terrier, who had walked in one day out of a summer storm. Mrs. Keil had called him Puppy because she didn't expect to keep him very long and she didn't want to impose a name on his next owner. Puppy stayed with the Keils for seven years—until he died of a heart attack two months before Mr. Keil died.

"I never would have thought to name her Dorold's Own

Starlet II, but she had the name already," said Mrs. Keil.

Early last year, said Mrs. Keil, she had taken Starlet to some local shows, by bus and subway, carrying her in a suitcase that weighed sixteen and a half pounds when the dog was inside. She had won some ribbons. At the Westminister show, Mrs. Keil had paid a professional handler to lead Starlet into the ring because she becomes nervous when the judges give her instructions.

Mrs. Keil seemed a little out of place at the Garden, surrounded by all the expensive-looking dogs with their expensive-looking people, a lady with an apron over her Pucci dress, the fresh-faced, outdoorsy girls in flat shoes, cardigan sweaters, and *Distemper Fighter* buttons.

I left Mrs. Keil for a few minutes and wandered over to a booth where a woman was selling expensive dog coats.

"We want her dog to look as smart as madame," the saleswoman was saying, holding up a pink cocktail coat of embroidered silk with a mohair lining.

I asked her, "When would a dog wear that?"

She raised her eyebrow and replied, "After five o'clock."

When I returned, Mrs. Keil was still on her wooden chair, peering down at Starlet, who was cuddling against her red skirt, froglike eyes alert, little curly piglike tail at rest. Mrs. Keil told me that Starlet has an electric-blue coat with a mink collar, but only wears it to keep warm.

A woman passed us and smiled down at Starlet. "Such a dood little dirl," she said. "She's so fat."

Mrs. Keil put on a pair of eyeglasses she had borrowed from a neighbor in Queens—her own were broken, she said —and looked at little fat Starlet.

"Oh, my goodness," said Mrs. Keil. "Maybe that's what the judges thought too."

IV

Winter Thoughts
of a Bush-League Ballplayer

Jerry Rosenthal is over thirty now, and the call will never come. Once, not so long ago, whenever the first soft fingers of spring stretched over the points of the city, Jerry Rosenthal would move nearer his telephone and frame his answer to the man who would say "We need a second baseman, kid. You available?"

He would wait, and he would think about his two and a half summers in the bush leagues, the boredom, the weariness, the long hours in a cramped station wagon, the poor pay, and the sparse crowds. He would remember a day in Lewiston, Idaho, when a ground ball skipped between his legs into the outfield, driving home the winning run. He had looked for a fat blade of grass to hide under.

But he would also remember a day in Yakima, Washington, sitting on the bench with a slow-healing broken cheekbone, when the manager sent him up to bat because everyone else was hurt or out of the game. He belted the second pitch into the left-field stands for a homerun.

"We need a second baseman, kid. You available?"

Sure, I'm available, he would have to say. I've been available since I was ten years old and imagined my face on a bubble-gum card, since summers in high school when I played on three different semipro teams at once, since the winter of 1960, when I signed a contract with the Milwaukee Braves on the dining-room table of my parents' home in Brooklyn.

Jerry Rosenthal was twenty-one at the time, and the future was a straight path to the Hall of Fame. He had one month to go at Hofstra University, where he had maintained a *B* average in class and a .408 average at bat. The contract carried a bonus of twenty-two thousand dollars, and when he signed it, his mother and sisters kissed him tearfully; his father, brother, and the scout shook his hand; and someone gave him a glass of Scotch. It tasted awful, he remembered.

And that was the start of his education.

"I was a gee-whiz kid," he told me one afternoon, years later. "All my life I'd thought about the glamour of professional baseball. I got to spring training in Georgia, and the food was lousy, and after you'd seen the movie, there was nothing else to do that week. But I learned the language."

He learned that year to call a baseball by its rightful name *(seed, pea, potato)* and that the worst accusation you can make of a ballplayer is that he chokes *(fails in the clutch).*

A fine thing to say to an umpire was "Shake yourself, meat, your eyes are stuck."

He was assigned to Eau Claire, Wisconsin, of the Northern League, a team that traveled in three station wagons. They would finish a night game in Duluth, Minnesota, at 11:30 P.M., be on the road by midnight, and reach Aberdeen, South Dakota, by 2 P.M. the following day. A poor sleeper in station

133

wagons, he became an authority on the Northern Lights.

"The next year I went to Yakima," he said, "and by this time I couldn't understand why people thought I led an exciting life.

"Baseball is three hours of tense excitement, but the rest of it is hanging around or traveling. I hate to play cards, and managers don't like players to go to the beach. You can see only so many afternoon cartoon festivals before you go out of your mind. I used to spend a lot of time reading in the public library. A lot of players thought I was crazy."

He became a little cynical, he said, about spitballs and emery balls and sign-stealing by telescope. He found out that bench jockeys weren't really vicious at all; they just made noise to keep themselves awake. He got into a lot of fights in Yakima because he had a manager who demanded that everyone run out on the field, swinging, after a bean ball. Anyone who stayed out of the brawl was fined fifty dollars. And he found out that fighting was kind of fun—it loosened everyone up.

He learned that the bullpen is the best place to pick up girls and that keeping one's mouth shut is a good general policy. There were a lot of pressures in the bush leagues and a lot of strange men living under them. He met some of the heroes of his Ebbets Field boyhood and was shocked by their skinny legs and potbellies and empty minds.

"Major league baseball players are not gods," he said. "They're just men in kids' uniforms."

He ran a strong, square hand through his reddish-blond

134

hair. "Baseball is a business, not a national pastime. People came out to the ball park on nights we had cow-milking contests and fireworks. When we were battling for first place, you could count the crowd between innings."

In the middle of the season at Yakima, Jerry was batting over .300 and fielding well. During pre-game practice one day, a thrown ball bounced into the dugout and smashed his cheek and jaw. After an operation, he was out of action for eight weeks. He never regained his form. When the Braves reassigned him to Yakima the following year, he refused to report. He felt he was ready for a team in a higher minor league. The Braves did not. Reluctantly they gave him his release. A free agent, Jerry went home to Brooklyn to wait.

We talked one afternoon that summer, while he was still waiting, and I asked him if it was all worth it—all the boredom and the weariness and the long hours—if the call never came and he never got his chance to play in the major leagues.

"It was worth every minute of it," he said. "An athlete learns a little more about life than an intellectual. You learn to hang in there, to keep going when you're so fouled up you think you'll die.

"Every day is another challenge. You've got to prove yourself all over again. You're at second base and a two-hundred-twenty-pound catcher comes barreling in to bust up the double play. You can't run away. You just jump and throw that ball right into his face, and if he doesn't get out

135

of the way, at least he'll never come in on you like that again."

He smiled. "A pitcher's struck you out five times, and you go up there knowing you can belt him. You made a bad error last inning, and now it's the crucial play of the game, and under your breath you ask the batter to hit the ball to you. That's hanging in there."

Jerry waited through the summer and through the following year, but the call did not come, and with each passing year the chance that it would ever come grew dimmer and dimmer until all hope was gone. Much later, we met at a boxing match. He had a good job and most of his bonus money, and he said he was very happy. A college graduate, a reader of books, he had spent summers in the bush leagues and learned to hang in there. He was way ahead of the game —except in the dying days of a cold hard winter, when the sky is streaked with springtime and the air is faintly touched with the smell of the outfield grass.

ANOTHER SEASON

I quit The New York Times *in the fall of 1971 to write novels. I knew I'd miss the quick excitement of deadline journalism; the tumble-rush after a hot story and the touchdown joy of reading it under my by-line only hours after I had written it.*

But I wanted more time to think about what I had seen during the past fourteen years, and more space to shape those thoughts into characters and stories.

I spent most of the next eleven years in the basement of my house writing books of fiction and nonfiction, movies, and television plays. Sometimes I longed for the sweaty flash of my old timetable life, but mostly I enjoyed a deeper, richer creative challenge. It was a wonderful time. I remember with pleasure the months of traveling slowly through the back roads of my imagination as I wrote such novels as One Fat Summer *and* Jock and Jill *and* The Summerboy.

I wasn't exactly a hermit for eleven years. I taught journalism in college. I visited schools where my books were being read. I spent thirteen weeks trying to write jokes for a TV variety show called "Saturday Night with Howard Cosell," *and I spent nine months on* The New York Post *writing a column about the people of the city. Those two jobs sent me back to the basement filled with new ideas for characters and stories.*

137

One special reward of those years was the easy-going extra hours I spent with my wife and my children.

In the summer of 1978 we learned that I had testicular cancer. Like most people, we regarded cancer as one of the most dread words in the language; if not a death sentence, we thought, at least it meant the end of a normal, productive life. We knew very little about cancer, but we learned quickly. After surgery, I underwent two years of chemotherapy. I was sick for a day or two after each treatment, and I lost some strength and some hair, but we were amazed at how normally my life continued: I wrote, I traveled, I swam and ran and played tennis. After the treatments were over, my strength and my hair returned. There was no evidence of cancer.

I was happy to be alive, to be enjoying my family, to be writing. As my children became teenagers, I told them of my old days roaming the country with a trusty portable typewriter on the trail of hot copy. It all seemed so very long ago. Sometimes it seemed as though it had all happened to someone else.

And then one day in the spring of 1982, Shad Northshield and Bud Lamoreaux, the executive producers of the CBS "Sunday Morning" show, asked me if I'd like to appear on television. It would mean hitting the road again and writing on deadline, learning a new field and meeting new people.

I thought of that day in 1962 when Jim Roach asked me if I'd like to go to Florida and cover the Mets' first spring training. It was hard to believe that was twenty years ago.

Joining "Sunday Morning" would be like starting all over again.

In the springtime, the beginning of a sportswriter's year.

138

I

Comeback Story

This is a comeback story without an ending. Whenever it seems as though Dan Lloyd has finally made it to that goal line in his head—or at least given up after a good try—the ball takes another crazy bounce. But whatever happens next, Dan Lloyd will always be coming back, coming on, growing and changing and trying to be better.

Dan Lloyd was twenty-six years old and a starting linebacker on the New York Giants when an opposing tight end slammed into his leg, tearing ligaments in his knee. That was around Thanksgiving, 1979. It was a typical football injury. Lloyd was finished for the season.

He bounced back from surgery and concentrated on getting ready for the next season. He ran and lifted weights. He had always believed that "hard work could make you a winner" and that the harder you worked, the sooner you would win. It was the traditional jock philosophy that had helped make him a football star at the University of Washington and he was convinced it would get him back into the NFL.

Now Lloyd envisioned himself the hero of a storybook comeback—*Linebacker Licks Ligament Surgery!*

Then one night in the spring of 1980, lumps popped out on his neck.

He actually welcomed them at first. Lloyd had always been sensitive about his neck, too long and too skinny, he thought, for a football player. He envied players with thick necks who could use their heads as battering rams without worrying about injury. In team pictures, he thought he looked like a giraffe. He told Vicki, his wife, "You know, if I just had some lumps on the other side, I'd have a great neck."

The lumps were swollen glands, the first symptom of a form of cancer called lymphocytic lymphoma. The disease struck just as Lloyd was beginning to reach his potential. His fourth season with the Giants was his best. He was an inside linebacker, 6 feet 2 inches tall, 245 pounds, fast and strong enough to smash through a line and sack a quarterback, to pursue a ball carrier and hammer him down. He was cocky and tough and he dreamed of becoming an all-pro and starring in a Super Bowl.

Now his body was the arena and the game was a deadly one between marauding killer cells and the toxic chemotherapy drugs that rushed through his system to seek and destroy them. He lost weight and strength and hair. In the beginning, he didn't think about coming back to football, merely of staying alive.

"Essentially, I felt my football career was over," he said. "I was concerned about my family. Vicki was pregnant with our second child. We were scared. And we didn't know anything about cancer."

Dan told me this in the backyard of his New Jersey home while we were taping my first interview for "Sunday Morning." Though cancer is a hundred different diseases with different treatments and different chances for recovery, Dan and I felt an immediate bond. In fact, I told him I remembered sitting next to him in the outpatient clinic waiting room of the Memorial Sloan-Kettering Cancer Center in New York. I didn't know who he was at the time. Just another guy waiting for treatment, I had thought, only bigger.

Lloyd approached his cancer the way he approached football. He gathered all the available information. He studied the options for treatment. He took responsibility for helping himself as much as possible. And he understood that doctors, like coaches, are human beings with specialized knowledge, not gods to be followed blindly.

Once again, he fell back on the discipline of the athlete. Hard work would get him through. He rode a stationary bicycle in the hospital and strode laps through the corridors, his intravenous bottles jiggling overhead on their metal perches. Between chemotherapy treatments, he exercised and he lifted weights. He concocted a little "physical bank account" fantasy for his workouts: Every mile he jogged, every pound he pumped, every minute he stretched and twisted was a deposit of health and energy into an account from which he could withdraw when the chemo made him sick and weak.

Meanwhile, the drugs were killing the cancer cells. The doctors at Memorial told him that his prognosis for a remission was good. Lloyd asked them if he might ever play football again. They hesitated because they had never faced such a situation before. But they could not think of a good reason to say no.

Another storybook comeback filled his head—*Linebacker Blitzes Cancer!*

Once Dan was convinced that he was going to live, he decided there was only one way he could prove to himself that he had beaten cancer—he would play pro football again.

The Giant team doctors were skeptical. They said that chemotherapy left the bones brittle and the muscles and organs more vulnerable to injury. They said that the wounds of people who underwent chemo were slower to heal.

The oncologist, a doctor specializing in cancer, said this was not true.

Sometimes Lloyd thought the team doctors were only looking for reasons to get rid of him. Sometimes he thought the oncologist was encouraging an impossible dream only to keep his spirits up during the treatments. But most of the time he believed that he would someday burst across the line of scrimmage again to stop an offensive play dead.

Lloyd's hopes of playing were raised and dashed again and again through the 1980 and 1981 seasons. Several times he thought he was close to suiting up, but the chemo drugs, administered intravenously every third week, weakened him and made it difficult for him to keep up his weight. Lloyd traveled with the team and tried to stay in shape. He appreciated the moral support of club officials. The defensive coach took an interest in him, and let him help out during practices. Lloyd planned to coach some day, and this was a good start.

But not all his teammates were pleased to have him around.

"Football players, as a group, don't like seeing guys that are injured or sick," he told me during the interview. "It's a head thing. It's your profession, you get hurt, you're out, your career is over. And they don't like to have that reminder around."

He grinned as he remembered sitting alone in the back of the team bus because nobody wanted to be near him. He shouted, "What's the matter, have I got cancer or something?" That lightened the situation. Several teammates came over and sat down next to him.

When the Giants opened their training camp in late July, 1982, Lloyd felt as fit as he ever had. He had prepared for camp by running the four miles from his home to the stadium, then running up and down the grandstand steps with a fifty-pound sandbag on his shoulder. Warmed up, he'd go under the stadium and pump iron.

He knew his chances of making the team were poor. The Giants linebacking unit was one of the best in football. He was twenty-nine, older than most players. Athletes rarely return to a major sport after a two-year absence for any reason, much less cancer. And few people shared his confidence.

But Lloyd was determined to play, if not for the Giants, then for another NFL team, and if not in the NFL then in the new United States Football League. As more people heard about his comeback attempt, he felt a greater pressure to succeed, not only for himself now, but for all those with cancer he could inspire to keep going.

"I'm representing a lot of people," he told me. "By the

same token, I don't want to set up unrealistic goals. I don't want to be out there come July twenty-third and not be able to play."

He looked fine on July twenty-third, the first full day of the Giants summer camp. He was one of the fastest in the 12-minute race, running more than one-and-three-quarter miles. He said he felt like the rookie Lloyd of six years ago who was so eager and idealistic the veterans nicknamed him "Spaceman."

On the third full day of camp, July 25, the comeback faltered. On a routine practice play, he tried to slide underneath a blocker. He drove his right knee into the ground. He heard a pop and his leg collapsed. He had torn cartilages. It wasn't as serious as the torn ligaments in his left knee that had sidelined him in 1979. Because of a new procedure called arthroscopic surgery in which the cartilage is removed through two small holes in the kneecap, Lloyd was working out again within three days. He hadn't come this far to quit now.

Maybe he went all out on the knee too early to prove to the coaches that he was worth their attention. Maybe the coaches pushed him along too fast because they needed an experienced linebacker for their practice sessions. In any case, still recuperating from that cartilage injury, Lloyd hurt his leg. The Giants sent him home.

I called him. He hadn't lost his tough humor. When I asked what his plans were, he said, "I'll be waiting for someone else to get hurt. Preferably an inside linebacker."

My profile of Dan Lloyd, titled "Wounded Winner," appeared on September 12, 1982, as scheduled. It was the first Sunday of the regular 1982 NFL season. I was proud of the story, and glad that it was my debut. I just wished that it had a happier ending.

A week later, the Giants placed Lloyd on the Injured Reserve list, which put him on the shelf for the season. He couldn't play for any other team. They paid his salary, though, which was $85,000, the most he had ever earned. At the end of that season Dan Lloyd announced his retirement from football. The Giants said he had no future with them, and Lloyd said it was time to get on with his long-term plan of becoming a coach. I remember reading that story and wondering if Lloyd felt sad or relieved now that his comeback dream was over.

I should have known better.

A month later, Lloyd and Vicki and their daughters, Jennifer Rae, who was five and a half, and Marcia Yuri, who was two, drove south. While his family toured Disney World, Lloyd tried out for the New Jersey Generals of the new league. He thought he was doing well, but he was also hearing those old whispers about his brittle chemo bones. When the Generals traded him to the Birmingham Stallions, Lloyd retired again.

But he had decided once that until he played pro football again, he had not beaten cancer. It didn't matter that the x-rays and the blood work and the physical examinations found no evidence of disease or that his doctors declared him

145

in remission, perhaps forever. Lloyd needed to pass a test of his own.

He wangled a tryout with the Washington Federals. He stayed with that club for seven weeks. He played, but he never started. He got credit for a few tackles and assists, but he wasn't satisfied yet. It wasn't good enough. He asked the Federals to release him so he could try to find a team that needed him.

He wrote letters and made phone calls and appeared on practice fields and in the offices of general managers. Most of the time, his letters were not answered and his phone calls were not returned and the men he went to see were too busy to talk to him for even a minute.

But he kept coming, picking himself up and starting again, shaking off his hurt and giving it another shot, just as he had been taught by every coach he had played under since he was a kid. He had something to prove to himself, the one person who would always know whether or not he had done his best.

And then, in May, he was wearing the uniform of the Michigan Panthers, the best team in the new league.

Suddenly, football was fun again. For the first time in three-and-a-half years he was playing with pleasure. He began on kick-off squads and as a substitute inside linebacker and he did well enough by his third game to be promoted to the starting team.

He had made it. He had come all the way back. He was a football player again. Finally, in his own mind, where it counted, he had beaten cancer.

146

Late in that game, bursting out of a three-point stance, his left hand snagged on the artificial turf. A finger bent, a tendon snapped. He was sent to Detroit for immediate surgery. A two-inch metal pin was hammered into his knuckle. He was out for the season.

When I talked to him, a few weeks later, I couldn't resist saying, "You give new meaning to the word irony. You make it all the way back from cancer and then you hurt your finger."

He agreed, laughing. "You know, that Michigan experience was wonderful. It reawakened my love of football. I feel like it's okay to go out on a high note like that."

His voice was light, positive. Vicki was pregnant with their third child, which signified to him that his body had renewed itself after the ravages of chemotherapy, which usually makes a man sterile.

He had sent out a number of letters requesting coaching jobs. He was willing to work as an unpaid assistant just to get his foot in the door.

He soon got a paying job as an assistant coach near his home. "It's more fun than playing," he told me. "You know, coaches have always been my role models, and I've always wanted to be a role model to young guys. And these kids are immensely interested, they really want to learn, and that really feeds your ego."

Dan and Vicki stayed up nights making charts for his defensive squad. But by the third week, the job began to go sour. Dan and the head coach could not get along. For the first time, Dan began to have serious doubts about himself and his life.

"I was driving home one evening, and I suddenly thought, 'What is it with me? Every time I hope, it gets stepped on. The Giants, the U.S.F.L., college coaching. Isn't it all right to hope? Isn't it all right to dream?'

"Then, suddenly, I guess you could call it like a religious experience, I was able to see everything crystal clear. And something in my mind said, 'You don't have to think it's your fault, that you did anything wrong. God has other plans for you. There is a meaning in your life. Just keep going, working hard. And you can hope.' "

By the time he was officially fired a few days later, he had called every pro coach and general manager he could think of and sent out another flock of letters.

And then in November, he signed with the Arizona Wranglers, a U.S.F.L. team coached by George Allen, who had a reputation of winning with older players who had been rejected by other teams. I congratulated him on the good news, and then asked, "By the way, you never did tell me whether or not you liked the piece I did on you."

"I guess it was real good from your point of you," said Lloyd, "but I hated the ending. I like happy endings, where the hero sacks the quarterback and wins the championship."

"Don't blame me for the ending," I said. "Maybe next time, you'll get it right."

Maybe no ending is the best ending for a Comeback Story.

II

Gerard Papa
Is a Tough Guy?

Gerard Papa grew up in the Brooklyn neighborhood that was a model for the locale of the film *Saturday Night Fever.* But Gerard Papa was never a finger-snapping, sharp-dressing, dancing dude.

He was small and shy and quiet. He came straight home from school to study. He got good marks. He never got into fights.

By the time I met him, though, Gerard Papa had the reputation of being a tough guy. How'd that happen?

"Bought a bomber jacket," says Gerard Papa, trying not to smile and spoil his image. "Started walking around like this." He stands up and swaggers around the room, rolling his thin shoulders under an imaginary bomber jacket. "Perfected the ghetto stare." He narrows his eyes and glares at me coldly.

"And people bought it?" I ask.

"There are gyms in Brooklyn right now they're afraid to see me walk in." Gerard Papa shakes with laughter. "Anybody knows me from before knows this is pretty funny."

Gerard Papa didn't set out to become a tough guy any more than he set out to become a saint with a basketball or a coach with a cause. In the beginning, all Gerard Papa wanted was a winning team.

He was eighteen years old, commuting to Columbia College from the home he shared with his widowed mother, a schoolteacher. He coached a church basketball team of fourteen-year-olds.

His team, which he named "The Flames," hadn't won a game all season when Gerard recruited a couple of Black teenagers from the Marlboro Projects, a lonely cluster of tall, stark apartment buildings in the middle of a predominately Italian neighborhood of private homes on neat, tree-shaded streets.

As near as they were, the Black kids of Marlboro rarely had anything to do with the white kids. The races were separated by an ocean of fear and ignorance. Blacks and whites shopped in different stores, went to different churches and mostly went to different schools. In the local high school, there was a "white" bathroom and a "Black" bathroom.

Gerard held his first integrated practice ten years ago, and he remembers it vividly. Blacks and whites were scrambling for the ball under a schoolyard basket when a van roared out of a sidestreet and came to a screeching halt outside the gate. A gang of white kids piled out, carrying baseball bats but no baseballs.

"I was driving a Thunderbird at the time," says Gerard, "and the Flames set the world's record for seven people getting into a Thunderbird. We took off. That was our first big chase. I figured if we could beat the van to Coney Island,

150

which is basically identified as a Black neighborhood, we'd be home free. They wouldn't follow us in there.

"We made it, but I realized we had a problem. I was kind of surprised. I mean, what was the big deal? It wasn't like I was trying to integrate the neighborhood. I just wanted to win a couple of games."

Gerard says he thought about disbanding his team every day for the next three years. He was threatened on the street and over the telephone. Most of the white boys on his team were pressured by their friends to quit. The Black boys were beaten up on their way to practice. The tires of his car were slashed. His mother begged him to give it up before he got hurt. But he wouldn't let the neighborhood put out the Flames.

Why, I ask him?

"Hey, I thought what we were doing was good, all right?" He gives me the ghetto stare, and when that doesn't work, he smiles. People have compared his dark, sharp-featured good looks to both Henry Winkler and John Travolta. "I was involved in something and I wanted to work it out. I don't like running away from a problem. It's no fun."

We are sitting in the bingo hall of the Roman Catholic Church of the Most Precious Blood, deep in the heart of Brooklyn, watching the opening game of the Flames' annual Christmas tournament. Since that car chase ten years ago, Gerard Papa has been graduated from Columbia College and the Columbia Law School. He went to work for a Wall Street law firm as a tax specialist and then gave up the job to open

151

a small neighborhood practice so he could stay close to the Flames.

Gerard's team of six kids has become an eight-team league of 300 kids, and "The Flames" has become the name for a youth program, a model of community self-help for the city and the nation.

"My own feelings changed a lot those first three years," says Gerard. "I didn't know anything about Black kids until they joined my team. And then, because all my troubles were coming from white kids, I viewed every Black guy as good and every white guy a problem, and then I matured and reached the stage where I don't notice anybody's color anymore."

Gerard taught himself to play tough and streety, to roll his shoulders and fire his ghetto stare, because it was the only way he could protect his players. He came to learn that most tough guys are phonies, and they were as scared of him as he was of them. He cajoled and begged and bullied his way into schoolyards and gyms and parish basketball courts for practice time for the Flames.

His first important breakthrough came when the priest at Most Precious Blood stood up for Gerard and offered his bingo hall as a home court.

The biggest breakthrough came when the Flames won the Catholic Youth Organization basketball championship.

Suddenly, it was chic to wear a T-shirt with the Flames logo of a Black hand and a white hand grasping a torch. It was not chic to give the Flames a hard time.

"A lot of people who doubted me and questioned me now believe in what we're doing," says Gerard, "and I think the answer is, if you're doing something that's good and you show people that you're going to stick with it and you're not going to half-step and you're not going to hold back and you're willing to do it for a long enough period and you're not going to be somebody who'll throw in the towel and say, 'Well, I tried,' then you're going to succeed."

The Flames have made it possible for white kids and Black kids to play basketball together now in neighborhoods where that would have once been impossible. But the Flames have not ended racism in Brooklyn. Not far from Most Precious Blood is a street called Avenue X. In 1982, Avenue X became a national symbol for racism when a Black transit worker stopped to buy a snack and was beaten to death by white Italian teenagers. Gerard organized a benefit game afterward to cool tempers and raise money for the widow. And he pressed on.

"What we got to do," he says, "is touch one kid, show one kid how to treat other people, and that rubs off on ten other kids. It's slow, but you can change the world, one kid at a time."

III

Tracee

Dawn breaks chilly and damp, and Tracee Talavera feels crummy. Her muscles ache, her throat is sore, she has a slight headache. She would like to stay burrowed in this warm bed in this cozy room crowded with five other girls and dozens of cuddly stuffed animals. From the muffled groans around her, she can tell that the others feel the same way.

She sits up. There are no days off on the road to the Olympics. Besides, she thinks, a crummy day may be just what she needs. She's been feeling too good lately. Maybe she needs the experience of working out while she feels bad.

That way, if she goes to a championship meet with a sore throat and a headache she'll be prepared. The difference between winning and losing in gymnastics is sometimes just a sneeze, a twitch, a frown. Maybe this lousy day will pay off.

The difference between Tracee Talavera and the millions of other teenaged girls who do gymnastics is more than muscle strength and balance and coordination. It is the willingness to get up at 4:45 A.M. no matter how she feels, and, perhaps even more important, the motivation to find a golden glimmer in a gray funk.

By 6 A.M., Tracee and the other young Elite (top competitive level) gymnasts who live together are limbering up for their daily work-out in a chilly, chalk-dusty gym in Eugene, Oregon. If Tracee is still feeling crummy, she isn't showing it. Once warmed up, she races across the gym, somersaults over a leather vaulting horse, and plunges into a pond of foam rubber.

She bounds to her feet and glances at coach Dick Mulvihill for approval. He turns away from Tracee to watch another girl.

Tracee's expression hardens, her eyes narrow. She jogs back to her starting position, waits until Mulvihill is looking at her, then starts again, charging down the narrow runway, leaping into the air, flipping over the horse. This time, as she rises from the foam, Mulvihill is nodding at her. Tracee smiles. She hurries away to try it again.

"She's hungry," says Mulvihill, a few minutes later. We are standing together in the gym as the camera crew shoots Tracee making an entry in the precise workout journal that every serious gymnast keeps. "She's the first one on the apparatus and just about the last to leave. She sets the pace for all the kids and she hustles all the time."

"Hunger, is that what you look for in a beginning gymnast?" I ask Mulvihill.

"I like to look at their eyes," he says. "If they're looking around and they sort of have a hungry, steely, squinty look, like they're sizing up the other girls."

"You sound like a prizefight manager," I say.

"I used to box myself," he says.

155

Six hundred miles away, Tracee's parents, Nancy and Rip Talavera, are just getting up. They think about Tracee every day, and their thoughts are mixed with pride and sorrow.

"Tracee went up to Eugene when she was eleven," says Nancy. "She's now sixteen. We've lost five years of her youth that we can never regain. It's a situation where you've given your child to someone else to raise and it's a loss."

Tracee calls home once a week from Eugene, and chitchats with her mother about grandma, the pets, neighbors. Nancy always felt it was important to keep Tracee up to date on family trivia so she wouldn't feel like a stranger when she came home. But Rip rarely talks to Tracee when she calls. He says it's too painful, he misses her so much. And Rip seems to be protecting himself from further hurt when he says, "In fact, when she does come back, it really is disappointing, because she's not the kid who left here." When I ask him about the eleven-year-old Tracee who left, his voice cracks. "That's like a dream."

Allowing Tracee to leave home was an emotionally painful decision, and an expensive one. It cost almost $10,000 a year in tuition and living expenses for Tracee to attend Mulvihill's National Academy of Artistic Gymnastics. And the decision was a gamble—balanced against the hope that Tracee would become a champion was the fear that she could be physically hurt or become psychologically stunted, a gym rat instead of a well-rounded person.

But the Talaveras had been heading toward that decision ever since Tracee was an infant, a nonstop crib bouncer, living-room rug flipper, a trampoline tumbler. She was pure energy looking for an outlet.

She found that outlet when she was five. Like millions of others around the world, she was captivated by Olga Korbut, the tiny gymnast from the Soviet Union who won a gold medal in the 1972 Olympics. Watching the Games on television, Tracee, and her sister, Coral, who was eight, determined to become gymnasts, too.

This wasn't as easy in 1972 as it would become a few years later when children's gymnastics classes sprang up like fast-food franchises. The Talaveras found no lessons available in San Francisco. They enrolled their daughters in acrobatics classes (after a year, the girls complained that the classes weren't "hard enough"), in ballet ("too slow"), and trampoline, before they eventually found a gymnastics club south of the city.

In the next few years, gymnastics came to dominate the Talaveras' family life. The girls moved up the levels of competition and their parents became their cheerleaders, chauffeurs, trainers. They searched for better coaching. They found a good coach in Walnut Creek, a suburb within driving distance of their San Francisco home. After a while, they moved to Walnut Creek.

During summer vacations, they traveled to Eugene so the girls could work out with Mulvihill and his wife, Linda Metheny, a gymnast in three Olympics.

Both sisters were strong and light for their body size, graceful, energetic, and talented. But Tracee had the kid

157

sister advantage of growing up with an older, more advanced gymnast; whatever Coral learned, Tracee learned, too. She also had what one Japanese coach called "konjo," an inner drive, a fighter's fire to keep going, to never quit.

In 1976, Nadia Comaneci of Rumania replaced Olga Korbut as the Olympic gymnastic darling and all over the world strong little girls fantasized about replacing Nadia. Tracee's potential was recognized. She was a California champion at nine, she was on track to the Olympic trials. Excitement grew in the Talavera household. If Tracee continued to develop, she might be the darling of the 1980 Olympics in Moscow. When the girls' Walnut Creek coach left California for a better job, Tracee and Coral went to live at the Academy in Eugene, to train full time with Mulvihill.

"She was the imp," remembers Mulvihill. "The vivacious little teeny-bopper that darted around and really didn't know what was going on but was having a good time."

Coral was injured and became discouraged. She left after a year. The Talaveras thought that Tracee would come home, too, but she stayed. She began winning local, state, and regional titles. She won two United States championships and a bronze medal at the World Games in Moscow. She won a place on the 1980 Olympic team.

She also seemed to flourish in the cloistered life of the Academy, a carefully regulated existence that allows no dating and hardly any activities beyond gymnastics and regular public school. Even school was bent around gymnastics. Tracee attended only three or four classes a day, mostly math, English, and foreign languages. She got credit for gym, music, art, and social studies because of gymnastics and the international travel—she got to China, Japan, and Europe even if she never got to the school cafeteria.

"Sometimes you wish you could go to dances and football games and people's parties and stuff," says Tracee, "but then you sort of think, well, I'm getting more out of life right now than they are and I can always go to parties later. So it's sort of . . . it's worth it, I think."

The girls of the Academy work out six days a week, three on the compulsory exercises that every gymnast must perform in competition, three days for the optional exercises that each performs to show off her own particular strength. Six hours a day of the vaulting horse and the tumbling mat and the uneven parallel bars and the balance beams, the endless floor routines practiced until each muscle has a memory of its own, pushing through pain and boredom and the low days when the coach scowls or, worse, ignores her, coming back after sprained ankles and pulled muscles and torn tendons and broken toes, ignoring the clouds of chalk dust and the chilly dawns and the constant "rips," the little skin tears in the palm of the hand that plague most gymnasts.

Many girls drop out of high-level competitive gymnastics, particularly those who have been pushed by their parents after their own interest waned. Some of those girls, afraid to confront their parents, will "eat their way out" of competition, or purposely get hurt.

Tracee's conflict was different. Her passion for gymnastics

159

was growing, even as her parents began to doubt that her life was taking the right course.

In the summer of 1980, Tracee's world came apart. First, President Carter canceled United States participation in the Olympics; there would be no trip to Moscow, no chance to become the first American female gymnast to ever win an Olympic medal, no shot at becoming the imp of the world.

Then, her father demanded that she leave the Academy and come home to stay.

"She was hooked on gymnastics, she wanted to do gymnastics at all costs," explains Rip now. He wanted her to concentrate on her studies so she could attend a good college. "Trace has to be prepared for life, and gymnastics isn't going to prepare her for life. It's a good experience in life, but it's not what's essential. Nobody is going to ask her how her double back was when she's looking for a job."

Tracee came home to Walnut Creek in the fall of 1980. She was fourteen. She never stopped nagging her mother and father to send her back to Eugene.

"She made it sufficiently tough," says Nancy, "that my husband and I let her go back. We wanted it to work so bad, but she didn't want it to work. She'd go to a local gym and she'd complain about everything."

Nancy's eyes filled with tears when she remembers the four months that Tracee was home. "She made us feel guilty that she wasn't doing her gymnastics in what she felt was the best place. Anytime there was a little problem, she'd say, 'Well, in Eugene we did it like this.' "

Nancy and Rip wanted Tracee to lead a "normal" life. But Walnut Creek wasn't "normal" for Tracee anymore.

"My gymnastics wasn't going anywhere," remembers Tracee. "I wanted to come back the whole time."

"She made it real impossible," says Rip. The final incident was a meet in Oakland, California. Coach Mulvihill was there, and Rip couldn't help noticing their easy rapport, how Tracee brightened up. After four months, Rip gave up and let Tracee return to Eugene.

"My dad just got sick of my nagging," says Tracee.

When she said that, she gave a little laugh. It sounded cold. I wondered how much guilt might be behind that little laugh. Tracee wanted to become the best that she could be, she obviously burned to be great. Her parents were ambitious for her, too. And yet, the pride they all felt was mixed with so much pain. They had all made sacrifices so Tracee could go for the gold.

When I interviewed Rip in the Fall of 1982, he said that he no longer pays any money to the Academy. Coach Mulvihill would not discuss his financial arrangements. But there was no doubt that Tracee was a prime attraction at the Academy. Her picture was on the cover of Academy publications, her poster was on sale in the office. The Academy has a local booster club of people who donate money.

I wondered how many Eugene girls attended classes at the Academy because Tracee was there. How many girls from other cities came to live at the Academy because they dreamed of becoming Olympians, too.

161

But staying there may be harder than getting there.

"It's not for everyone," says Tracee. We're sitting in the upstairs living room of the Mulvihill house rather than the downstairs lounge area of the dormitory, because one of the girls is sick and we don't want to disturb her. The interview, one of an increasing number that Tracee undergoes, is just an interruption in this day that broke chill and damp and crummy. After her workout, she lifted weights, jogged, and went to school.

Meanwhile, six hundred miles to the south, Rip and Nancy are thinking about her, wishing they were there to monitor her studies, wondering if the Mulvihills care as much about her life outside gymnastics as they do.

Rip thinks about the addiction to glory, and what will happen to her psyche and her body as she pounds away toward the next Olympics. Nancy thinks about what will happen to her when her gymnastics career is over.

"I've seen a lot of kids who haven't had the same success they had as a gymnast feel they're a failure," she says. "A couple of kids have gone anorexic because they're still striving to be that cute little gymnast that they were at eleven and twelve and thirteen and now they're seventeen and they're not getting that attention."

The family is still deeply involved in gymnastics. Coral coaches at her college, Nancy judges meets, and Rip teaches at a small local club. He says he is more relaxed with other peoples' daughters than he ever was with his own.

"So I lose Tracee," he says, glancing around the gym, "but

I got about thirty other kids here that I work with. So these are like my, you know, almost like my family."

Nancy nods when I ask her if she ever thinks about that decision they made years ago to let their daughters become gymnasts, and the decisions that followed to let Tracee devote her life to it. "She had a talent and we were lucky enough to be able to let her pursue it. I don't think what we've done would be much different than what most parents would do. Most parents want to do what's best for their kids. And I feel that's what we've done."

Back in Eugene, Tracee does her homework, has supper with the other girls, then watches some television, "General Hospital" or another soap taped earlier in the day. She will go to sleep early. She has to get up tomorrow morning at 4:45.

"Some girls just can't take it," said Tracee when I saw her. "First of all, they're used to their own rooms. They're used to, like, having the whole room, everything of theirs and they get this little space."

She talked about the trouble she has readjusting to her parents' house when she returns a few times a year on brief vacations.

"It's really weird going back home," she says. "You know, here, all fourteen of us go here, then all fourteen go there. It's done in such large groups and like at home I'm sort of by myself a lot. And you know, there's only four people in my family so its just like, gosh it's so empty you know, there's no one there."

163

But in June of 1983, Tracee responded to her parents' wishes and came home again. Her grandmother was dying and her father, Rip, was more upset than ever by Tracee's absence.

Tracee settled into the life of the family. She spent the summer working out in the gym where Rip volunteered. She still planned to try out for the Olympic team.

Was Tracee going to stay home this time? The last time I called, her mother's voice sounded uncertain as she said, "I'm keeping my fingers crossed."

IV

On the Road Again

ATLANTIC CITY—Mickey Mantle and I are taping an interview in the hotel-casino for which he now does public relations. He pushes his drink aside and says, "My only regret is that I didn't take better care of myself."

When I ask Mantle what he means, specifically, he becomes restless in his chair, looks around, mumbles something about not doing enough leg exercises back in 1951. When I persist, he puffs himself up like a bully-fish and snaps, "Let's close it off, haven't you got enough?"

I have an instant flashback: It's 1960, I'm a twenty-two-year-old rookie reporter at *The New York Times*, nervous and very polite as I ask Mantle a question before a game at Yankee Stadium. Viciously, he curses me out. For a long time, I felt badly about that and wondered what I had done wrong. Eventually, I found out that Mantle was insecure himself in those days, and sometimes acted like a jerk. But I never quite forgave him.

Maybe that's why my voice has a sharp edge now in 1983 as I ask, "Are you in a hurry, or is this line of questioning bothering you?"

That lets some of the air out of Mantle. He relaxes. And soon he is telling me how he never stayed in shape during the off-season, how he went back to Oklahoma and drank all winter, how poor training habits stole years and hits from his career.

During the 1960s, he says, he even drank during the season, mostly out of boredom.

"My wife and kids didn't come to New York with me," he says. "And I stayed in a hotel and from the time the game was over till the next day there wasn't very much for me to do, you know, except I would go out to eat and I would start drinking, you know. I think it was just from monotony, from just not having anything else to do."

He might have been up in the record books with Stan Musial and Hank Aaron, he says, guys who took care of themselves. His voice is full of regret. For the first time, I begin to like this graying golden boy.

* * * *

NEW YORK—"I always wanted to be close to my father," says Nancy Lieberman, the high school, college, Olympic, and professional basketball star. "When I didn't get that attention when I was younger, it made me just get into a little shell and I rejected a lot of suggestions that my family had. I always wanted to prove that I could do it on my own.

"My mother would tell me, 'You're never going to make anything of yourself playing basketball, that's a boys' sport.

We want you to be a nice young lady.'

"I said, 'Mom, I'm not taking drugs. I'm not mugging people. I'm not running away from home. All I'm doing is playing sports. So I'm in the schoolyard eight hours a day with the guys. There's nothing wrong with it, 'cause I'm not hurting anybody. I like it, I enjoy it, it's healthy.'

"This was my attitude. It's really ironic because, you know, now my mother is my biggest fan. I mean, she's at every game and she calls me, 'Are you practicing?' I say, 'No, Mom, I was tired.' She says, 'Get out there and practice.' Where before, she was the one who was puncturing my basketballs."

Nancy Lieberman, who hopes to do for women's pro basketball what Billie Jean King did for women's pro tennis, is so bright and lively and talks so fast, that it takes an instant before her last words register and I ask, "Puncturing the basketballs?"

She laughs. "I had about seven basketballs and I would just want to go out and play all the time and my mother finally said, 'No more, you're not going out.' And I would stay in the house and I'd dribble the ball around the house and I'd jump up and touch the ceiling and she just got so annoyed at me, she took a screwdriver one day and started popping my basketballs.

"I was so upset. The only thing I ever spent my paper route money on was sports equipment. She'd puncture one, I'd have another."

I ask Nancy when her mother came around.

"We finally worked it out when I was chosen for the Olympic team," says Nancy. "That's when she realized that there was a future for me and I wasn't the only female playing basketball."

* * * *

ATLANTA—"A lot of people ask me," said Dutch Rennert, one of the best umpires in the National League, " 'How can you call strikes on a fellow who makes a million dollars a year?'

"Well, that's his problem, he makes a million. I'd like to make a million. I don't. But a ball's a ball and a strike's a strike."

I asked him if his mind ever wandered during a game.

He laughed. "I'll probably never be a great umpire, because if I see a beautiful blonde walking in the stands, I say, 'There's a beautiful blonde.' There goes my concentration.

"Sometimes my mind does wander. I think about home, about my wife, the grandchildren, the weather. That's lack of concentration."

Delighted with that taped proof that umpires were human, I went up to the pressbox at Braves' Field to visit with some of my old newspaper friends. Before the game, they had teased me about leaving dear old print journalism for "electronic" journalism.

I hadn't been in a baseball pressbox for many years, and

168

I stood in the doorway a long time before I figured out what seemed so different to me.

It was too quiet.

I missed the tickety-click of the little typewriters we used to carry around the league. Everyone was using word-processors, micro-computers linked to their offices by telephone.

Suddenly, one of the reporters yelled, "I'm down!"

"Me, too," shouted another.

There were curses and moans up and down the pressbox. The electric power had failed, and a dozen computers had blinked off. The stories being written simply vanished off the screens.

I imagined all my old friends' words rising into the atmosphere like smoke before they disappeared forever.

"Electronic" journalism, indeed. I tried not to smile.

* * * *

CULVER CITY, CALIFORNIA—The most romantic of Olympic love stories began at the Melbourne, Australia, Games in 1956 when Olga Fikotova of Prague, Czechoslovakia, met Harold Connolly of Boston, U.S.A. She was a discus thrower. He hurled the hammer.

They fell in love. They each won a gold medal. They married, came to America, and had four tall, strong children, two girls and two boys.

Harold and Olga were teachers. They encouraged their

169

children to be athletic, but never at the cost of music or literature or schoolwork or being humane, caring people.

Their love story ended sometime in the 1970s, in Culver City, which is part of Los Angeles. According to Harold, they divorced because of "women's liberation." According to Olga, it was the common matter of two people growing up and growing apart.

"He was like an apple pie and I was like rocky road ice cream," was the way Olga explained it to her children and, later, to me. "Apple pie and rocky road ice cream are very good separately, but they don't mix."

But the story continues. All four children are athletic, and one of them, Merja (pronounced Maria), hopes someday to make the Olympic volleyball team. She is six feet tall, a star of the U.C.L.A. team.

When I asked Olga how she felt about another Olympic gold medalist in the family, she said: "It's not that I want another Connolly in the Olympics, that's childish. But I do want Merja to have an experience that has made something out of me internally."

And when I asked Merja the same question, she said: "I would never want people to think of me as Merja Connolly, the athlete. Or, you know, that volleyball player. I'd like them to think of me first as, yeah, that great person, Merja Connolly, that great friend."

* * * *

RENO, NEVADA—I have waited more than a dozen years to meet Tom Meschery and ask him this question.

"Once, I read that you threatened to kill a guy who called you a 'pansy poet.' How come? I mean, if a six-foot six-inch National Basketball Association all-star with a reputation as a tough enforcer is insecure, what chance do the rest of us have?"

Meschery's fierce moustache twitches as he smiles, and his gentle eyes laugh. He's a coach, not a player now, but he's still a poet.

"I wasn't so resentful for myself," he says, "but for the idea of poetry. Why should poets have to defend themselves? Aren't we all a mixture of masculine and feminine? Shouldn't we be proud of that? And it has nothing to do with sex. It's a shame that such ideas still float around, and I'd like to help eliminate them, just so kids can write poetry without ever worrying what people might say."

* * * *

ROCKPORT, MASS—Dressed as a boy, Bobbi Gibb "stumbled from the bushes into the midst of runners, wondering how many other women writers, artists, historians, scientists, soldiers had to disguise their femininity so well that history has not yet still discovered."

That was from her memoir of the 1966 Boston Marathon, called *To Boston With Love.* Bobbi Gibb was twenty-three

171

years old then, a small, slim blond woman who had always run fast as a girl. She was furious to learn that women were not allowed to run the 26-mile 365-yard distance. So she ran it in disguise, the first woman to run the race. Some men running near her discovered her secret.

"They thought it was great," she remembers. "I could tell by the way they said, 'Gee, I wish my girlfriend would run.' You see, they really wanted to share this, because they loved running."

Bobbi Gibb never became a famous runner. She was ahead of her time. She got married, moved to California, got divorced, married again, bore a child, became a lawyer and a writer and sculptor.

In 1983, at the age of forty, she ran in the Boston Marathon again. Not only did she run as a female this time, but she was hailed and applauded as a true forerunner, a person who had helped blaze a trail for others.

In 1983, not only were women running proudly in the Boston Marathon, but handicapped athletes in wheelchairs were competing.

And world-class women runners were looking forward to 1984, when women would run the marathon distance for the first time in the Olympic Games.

I visited Bobbi Gibb in her home in Rockport. We talked about her childhood, how she loved to race along the beach, faster than all her friends, and that first marathon she ran as an outlaw. And we talked about a forerunner's dream.

"My dream was that men and women could run together

and share the consciousness of that common bond of humanity based on mutual committment. Hatred, war between the sexes exhaust both and lead to nothing."

* * * *

NEW YORK—I always liked Joe Namath; he was honest and he delivered. In 1969, as promised, he led the Jets to victory in the Super Bowl, and in 1983, after carefully preparing himself in acting classes and in regional theaters, he appeared on Broadway in *The Caine Mutiny Court-Martial.* Joe's performance as Lieutenant Maryk was solid and professional.

A few days after I saw the play, I asked him about the rare chance he had of excelling in two careers—football and acting—in one lifetime.

He shook his head. "I don't think it's going to happen. Football was my ticket out of Beaver Falls, Pennsylvania, it was my chance to escape the steel mills. I don't have those drives and hungers anymore. I like my comforts. I don't think I could dedicate myself to my work so exclusively again."

His green eyes danced. "But, who knows? Maybe if the right roles come around. . . ."

* * * *

NEW PALTZ, N.Y.—As a young boy, Floyd Patterson scurried through the meanest streets of Brooklyn like a gutter rat. He lived in subway tunnels and he ate stolen food. He says now that he was saved from an early death by a special school for emotionally disturbed children and by boxing.

He was the first boxer I ever interviewed. I was working the midnight shift as a rewrite reporter when I got a telephone tip from my father that Floyd Patterson was going to make a surprise visit the next morning to his old school.

My father was the director of those schools for the New York City Board of Education. Patterson had just regained his heavy weight championship from Ingemar Johansson of Sweden, who had beaten him the year before.

I was very impressed with Patterson, his intelligence, his dignity, the kindly and supportive way he talked to the kids. He presented a trophy and said: "I'm proud to bring back the championship to America and to P.S. 614."

I was disgusted a few years later, in 1965, when Patterson proclaimed himself the defender of Christianity, Goodness, and the American Way in a championship match in Las Vegas against Muhammad Ali, a recent convert to the religion of Islam. I was also disgusted by the way Ali mocked and humiliated Patterson, and beat him slowly and cruelly. But I couldn't quite feel sorry for Patterson. What right did Patterson have to make a boxing match into a Holy War?

Over the years, I thought about those two Pattersons, the one I liked at P.S. 614 and the one I didn't like in Las Vegas.

174

In both cases, he was speaking out of his own sense of patrio-
tism and what he thought was right. Could he have been
right both times or wrong both times? Could he have
changed, could I have changed? Can something be right in
one situation and wrong in another?

I was still thinking about those questions in 1983, when I
sat in the handsome living room of the stone country house
Patterson shares with his wife and his daughters. He was a
businessman now, but he had stayed in boxing in a meaning-
ful way. He was a New York State athletic commissioner
particularly concerned with boxing safety, and he ran a free
boxing club in his barn. Most of the boxers were local young
men. He was like a father to several of them. It was his way
of paying back.

We talked for several hours. I was impressed again by his
intelligence, his dignity, and his caring. He said that he had
never shaken free of the insecurities of his childhood; deep
down, he said, he was still the suspicious, fearful, dirty boy
of the gutter. Whenever he saw a boy who reminded him of
himself, he tried to reach out, to give him a chance to dream
and to make his dreams come true. Sometimes, he even
brought them into his house. He had adopted one such boy.

I thought of Ali, eighteen years ago mocking and beating
this man when Ali was the champ and Patterson was the
pathetic has-been.

Now, Patterson, the beaten, was living a full, rich life,
surrounded by loved ones, doing good.

Ali, the victor, seemed to be sliding into oblivion. There

175

had been reports in the press that Ali had suffered brain damage from his fights. His speech did seem thicker these days. Watching him on television, I had felt sad at how much slower and duller he seemed. There were rumors that he was taking drugs.

People were saying how quickly yesterday's champ becomes tomorrow's chump.

But I'm not writing him off so fast.

Patterson's story proves there's always hope. Until the final bell sounds, you can still get off the floor and reverse the decision.

* * * *

BERKELEY, CALIFORNIA—Harry Edwards and I are sitting in a waterfront restaurant, talking about old and new times. I'm glad to see him again. Of all the people I've met in sports, he has been one of the most admirable and humane and consistent.

Fifteen years ago, when we first met, he was a young college instructor organizing the Olympic Committee for Human Rights. He was trying to awaken America to the racism in sports as a symptom of so many injustices that we must struggle against to overcome.

Among his students at San Jose State then were Tommie Smith and John Carlos, who raised their black-gloved fists at the 1968 Olympics. They were immediately thrown out of

176

the Olympic Village. Edwards, Smith, and Carlos were branded as dangerous radicals.

Now Smith is a college track coach, Carlos works for the Los Angeles Olympic Organizing Committee, and Edwards is a famous and highly respected professor of sociology at the University of California, at Berkeley.

But the struggle continues.

Fifteen years ago, I remind him, the big stories in sports were the abuse of drugs, the exploitation of college football players, and the political manipulation of international athletic events.

Look what's in the news these days. Cocaine and steroids. Star college athletes who can't read or write. Boycotts against South African teams.

"Don't ever get discouraged," says Harry. "One person isn't going to solve all the problems of the world. Nobody's going to wake up one day and bring peace and end disease.

"But one person CAN make a difference. Just keep working in your own little area. For me that's sports. For someone else, a community. It doesn't matter how narrow your area might seem. Just keep at it, do the best you can. Try to leave the world a little better than when you found it."